Tough-Luck Karen

Also by Johanna Hurwitz

Aldo Applesauce
What Goes Up Must Come Down
(hardcover title: *The Law of Gravity*)

**Other APPLE® PAPERBACKS
you will want to read:**

The Cybil War
    by Betsy Byars
Dreams of Victory
    by Ellen Conford
The Pinballs
    by Betsy Byars
The Two-Thousand-Pound Goldfish
    by Betsy Byars
With a Wave of the Wand
    by Mark Jonathan Harris

Tough-Luck Karen

by
Johanna Hurwitz

Illustrated by
Diane de Groat

AN
APPLE®
PAPERBACK

SCHOLASTIC INC.
New York Toronto London Auckland Sydney

ISBN 0-590-41118-7

12 11 10 9 8 7 6 5 4 3 2   7 8 9/8 0 1/9

Printed in the U.S.A.   28

For Suzanne Ruta.
It's good luck
that she is my sister.

Tough-Luck Karen

Contents

1.

Karen-
Caren-
Karyn

Karen Sossi sat on her bed and reread the letter
that she was holding. It said:

Dear Friend,
    This is a chain letter approved by the U.S.
Post Office as an educational game. Please
send a picture postcard to the first person on
the list below. Then copy this letter and send
it to six friends. Leave the first name off the
list, advance the others up one space, and add
your name to the bottom of the list. This

11

chain has not been broken since January 1, 1972. In eighteen days you will receive 500 postcards from all over the world. If you don't have the letters in the mail in three days, the chain will be broken. *If you break the chain you will have seven years of bad luck!*

Five names were listed on the page. The fifth

one, the person who had sent the chain letter to Karen, was Holly Whitestone, a girl who had been in Karen's English class when she still lived in New York City.

Ten months ago, when the Sossi family had moved to New Jersey, Karen's old English teacher had put Karen's new address on the blackboard to encourage the class to keep in touch with her. Holly had not been a friend of Karen's, and she had never written before. Now, in addition to the copy of the letter from Holly, Karen had two more copies of the same letter. They had been sent by two other girls from that same class, Gloria Goodman and Nina Kraft. Obviously they had all been searching for names at the same time.

Karen sighed. It was Sunday evening, and there were two good programs that she wanted to watch on TV. But although she had only been in eighth grade a month, the homework was already piling up. Karen didn't know how she would survive the school year. She had to make a decision. Should she try to do her math homework, or should she answer the chain letters?

Karen loved getting mail. She had half a dozen pen pals living in countries all over the world. She wrote them long and frequent letters and eagerly awaited their answers. But from past experience she knew that chain letters were an exercise in futility. Whenever she sent out the letters and waited for the results, nothing happened. She had never received more than two postcards, even though she was always promised hundreds. Karen turned to her math book. In four weeks of school, Mrs. Nesbitt had never once forgotten to collect the homework. Karen sighed and decided she would risk seven years of bad luck by ignoring the chain letter. After all, even if she took three days to send out the eighteen copies that the three letters asked for, she would still be using time she needed for her schoolwork, and she would have bad luck on the math test the day after tomorrow.

She took a sheet of loose-leaf paper and wrote her name neatly in the right-hand corner. "Karen Sossi," she wrote, experimenting and writing the *K* with a fancy loop. She studied her signature. It looked slightly better than usual, but not good enough. She wished her name was spelled with a *C*. Caren Sossi seemed more interesting, less common and more distinctive. There were so many other ways one could spell her name: Karyn, Karin, Carin, Caren, Caryn. Why did her parents have to choose the dullest way of all? She tried writing the alternatives: "Miss Caren Sossi. Ms. Caren Sossi, Ms. Caryn Sossi. Ms. Carin Sossi." Kara was a nice name too, unusual but not too gross. In Karen's class in New York, there had been one girl whose parents had named their daughter Pocahontas Goldhirsch. Poor Pokey! Karen remembered her. Tomorrow she would probably get another chain letter from her. She was a slowpoke, like her name.

Karen looked at the sheet of loose-leaf paper. Without realizing it, she had half covered the page with variations of her name. She took out a clean sheet and began again. "Karen Sossi," she wrote, forgetting to make the fancy loop on the *K*.

She opened her math book to page 49, where the assignment was. "Draw a graph," it said.

"Auggg," moaned Karen, and she threw the math book against her bedroom door in disgust.

"Hey, what's up?" called Aldo, her younger brother. He charged into her room without knocking.

Karen looked at him and remembered how sweet it was to be nine years old. Life had been so simple in those days. There hadn't been much homework and certainly none needing graph paper. School was like one big game when you were in fifth grade.

"I have to draw a graph for my math homework, and I forgot to buy graph paper over the weekend," she said.

"Maybe Elaine has some," suggested Aldo, and he went charging off to the room of their fourteen-year-old sister, who was in ninth grade.

"Don't you dare come in here without knocking," Elaine shrieked.

Karen sat on her bed, too dejected to go to Aldo's defense.

Aldo returned. "Sorry," he said. "She doesn't have any." He thought a moment. "Is there anyone in your class who lives nearby that you could borrow the paper from?"

"No," said Karen. Unlike Aldo and Elaine, she had not made any real friends since she moved to Woodside, New Jersey.

"I'll go ask Mom," said Aldo. "Maybe she has an idea." Aldo rushed out of the room. Karen sat numbly looking at the sheet of loose-leaf paper. How could she have been so stupid? They had been doing graphs in class on Friday, and Mrs. Nesbitt had told them to buy some paper over the weekend. Nothing would be open at this hour. She really had rotten luck.

Aldo returned. "Mom says could you draw lines

on a piece of regular paper and make your own graph paper?" he asked.

"That's crazy," said Karen. "It would take hours."

Aldo bounced out of the room. Karen tried to remember how it was to be young and have that sort of energy. She couldn't. She had been nine too long ago. Four years!

She didn't even have the energy to go into the living room and ask her mother to write a note excusing her from the assignment. She could say that they had been away for the weekend, which they hadn't; or she could say that Karen had sprained her wrist, which she hadn't; or she could say that their dog had chewed up all the graph paper in the house. The teacher wouldn't have to know that they didn't own a dog.

Mrs. Sossi walked into Karen's room. The door had been left open by Aldo, so she didn't even need to knock. "Karen, why do you always leave everything till the last moment?" she asked.

"It's not the last moment," Karen retorted. "It's two hours till my bedtime. It should have been plenty of time to do my homework, and I would even have had time left over for TV."

"But you are so careless these days," said her

mother. "Is there any homework that doesn't need graph paper that you could be doing?"

"No," said Karen.

"What are you going to do?" asked her mother.

"You could write me a note," suggested Karen.

"Karen, I wrote two notes for you last week," Mrs. Sossi reminded her. "When you gave me that box of stationery for Mother's Day, I had no idea that it would be used up so quickly. I wrote one note asking that you be excused from swimming with your gym class because you lost your bathing suit. Then I had to write another note asking for an extension for your book report because you left the book in your locker at school and couldn't finish reading it. You can't go through life asking me to write notes for you."

"Just one more," pleaded Karen. "After this, I'll be more careful. I promise."

"Give me a sheet of paper," said Mrs. Sossi. "Considering that you are the letter writer in this family, I'm the one who is getting to have all the pen pals."

Karen knew that her mother was referring not only to the school notes she had written but also to the couple of warnings that she had received from teachers since the new school year had begun.

She couldn't seem to make her parents understand that none of the schoolwork seemed very important to her. What was the purpose of book reports or learning how to make graphs? In all her thirteen years, she had never seen her parents sit down and make a graph to help them in any way.

Mr. Sossi joined them in Karen's room. "What's the problem?" he asked.

"The usual," Mrs. Sossi said with a sigh.

"Dad," said Karen. "I have a question to ask you."

"Fire away," said Mr. Sossi.

"Well," said Karen, "just tell me this. Did you ever in your life have to make a graph? Do you ever make them at work? This is a dumb assignment. Almost everything we learn at school is a waste of time, but graphs are probably the worst."

"Now wait a minute, Karen," said Mr. Sossi. "That's unfair. Graphs are very important."

"Give me an example of when you ever made one."

"Well, uh, uh. . . ." Mr. Sossi said, trying to answer the question.

"See? I knew you never used them. I bet you never made a single graph in your entire life," said Karen.

"How much do you want to bet?"

"A quarter," said Karen.

"You lose," said Mr. Sossi. "I made plenty of graphs in my time. When I was in eighth grade like you, I must have made dozens of them—bar graphs, line graphs, all sorts."

"That doesn't count if you made them for school," yelled Karen. "I was right, and you owe me a quarter."

Mr. Sossi laughed and stuck his hand into his pocket, looking for change.

"Nevertheless, it's still a good skill to have," he said. "And you have to know how to read graphs. You often see them in newspapers."

"How boring," Karen said, sighing. "It's not as useful as cooking." Cooking was a skill that she worked at and enjoyed very much. That very afternoon she had made an apple pie, which the family had devoured at supper.

"Perhaps you should write to Julia Child and ask her if she ever makes graphs," said Mr. Sossi. Karen never missed a chance to see Julia Child teach cooking on television.

"You can't eat graphs," said Karen.

Aldo came charging back into Karen's room. "Look," he said proudly and handed her a sheet of paper. He had taken a ruler and drawn lines in both directions on the page. But the spacing between the lines was uneven, and some of the lines were crooked, despite the use of the ruler.

"I can't use this," complained Karen. "It's lousy."

Aldo's usually cheerful face clouded.

"That was nice of you, Aldo, to try and help Karen," said Mrs. Sossi, putting her arm around Aldo's shoulder.

"Thank you, Saint Aldo," said Karen.

"That's enough, Karen. I think you are over-tired," said Mrs. Sossi. "You had better get ready for bed since you can't do your homework."

"I thought I'd watch some TV," said Karen.

"Not tonight," said Mrs. Sossi. "I want your light out in fifteen minutes."

Suddenly the mob of people was gone, and Karen was alone in her room. She felt awful. She didn't know if it was because she hadn't done her math homework or because she couldn't watch TV. She tried to figure out what had made her feel so terrible, and she realized it was Aldo. She looked at the sheet of imitation graph paper on her bed. He really had meant well. She heard other kids talking about their little brothers and sisters, and she knew that as far as brothers were concerned, she was very lucky. Sometimes she had fights with Elaine, but she rarely had any disagreements with Aldo. He was too sweet and good-natured. He was an unusual kid, she thought. Really, he *was* a saint. But sometimes it was hard to live with such a perfect person, especially if one felt less than perfect oneself. He made her look even worse than she was.

Karen tore Aldo's graph paper into shreds. Then she picked up the three copies of the chain letter and reread one once again. Although she still had another day, because the letters had arrived on Saturday, they were already causing her bad luck. I'm not superstitious, she told the letters, as she tore them to pieces. Grimly she tore the little pieces into still smaller shreds. Then a thought crossed her mind. Perhaps because she had received three letters she would get three times seven years of bad luck. Twenty-one years! Ugh.

As she began undressing for bed, Karen decided that tomorrow she would write her name on all papers as Carin. Perhaps things would go a bit better for a girl named Carin Sossi. She was tired of being Karen.

2.

Bad Luck

Perhaps it was because she had torn up the chain letters, perhaps it wasn't, but the next week was filled with more misfortune than most people could expect in a month, or maybe even a year. Karen's bad luck began on Monday morning when she dropped half of an English muffin, butter side down, naturally, on her gray wool slacks as she sat at the breakfast table. She had to rush to change her clothes and then had to run to catch the school bus, and she narrowly missed being late.

In school, she remembered that she had put a

five-dollar bill in the pocket of the gray slacks for expenses on a class trip. Ms. Drangle, the teacher leading the trip, was annoyed to have to lay out the money for Karen. The trip was to Rutgers University to visit the science labs there. Most of the class was thrilled by the prospect of spending a day in college. The experience did not please Karen. It only served to remind her that after four years of high school she might have to undergo four years of college. And besides, all day she kept thinking about her money in her pants pocket back at home. When she returned home, she rushed to retrieve the five-dollar bill.

"Where are my gray slacks?" she asked her mother.

"There's very efficient service around here," said Mrs. Sossi. "I dropped them off at the dry cleaners when I was doing errands this morning."

"Did you take the money out of the pocket?" asked Karen.

"What money?" asked Mrs. Sossi.

"The money in the pocket," shrieked Karen.

"I didn't know there was anything in the pocket."

"Five dollars of my birthday money," moaned Karen. "I spent three dollars and forty-five cents in the cafeteria at Rutgers on the trip today, and I have to pay it back to Ms. Drangle."

Mrs. Sossi didn't answer Karen. She went to the telephone and dialed the number of the dry cleaners. "Could you check the pockets of a pair of slacks that I brought in this morning? I believe I left some money in one of them."

There was a pause, and Mrs. Sossi nodded her head, although the person at the other end of the line could not see her. "Thank you very much," Mrs. Sossi said. She turned to Karen. "They say that they always check all pockets when clothing is brought in," she explained.

"Well, someone is lying," said Karen, "and that someone is richer by five dollars. My five dollars. And they say that crime doesn't pay!" She sniffed.

"Karen, I'll lend you the money to pay back Ms. Drangle. But you have to learn to be more careful. If you were more careful, you wouldn't have dropped anything on those slacks this morning in the first place," said Mrs. Sossi.

That blow was just the beginning of the week. Things got worse.

On Tuesday afternoon, Mrs. Sossi gave Karen two letters to mail and a five-dollar bill and asked her to pick up a half-gallon of milk at the delicatessen. Karen went off, dropped the things in the mailbox, and didn't notice until she was in the delicatessen that she was holding a letter in her hand and not a five-dollar bill. When she arrived home without the milk and still holding the second, unmailed letter, Mrs. Sossi reacted with exasperation.

"Karen, we can't afford to keep you at this rate. Go back to the mailbox and mail this other letter and just wait for the postal truck. It comes to collect the mail around five o'clock. Explain to the driver what happened, and he'll give you the money back."

Karen felt like an absolute idiot standing guard in front of the mailbox. Several people came by to post letters, and she tried to act as if she were just casually waiting for someone. She wondered how many letters were covering her five-dollar bill by now. One woman was obviously giving a party, because she stuck at least three dozen mint-green envelopes into the box together. Perhaps she sent out her Christmas cards very early, thought Karen. Halloween hadn't even come yet.

Aldo rode by on his bicycle on his way home from playing at a friend's house. "Hey, why are you standing here?" he wanted to know.

"It's a long, sad story, like the whole of my life," said Karen.

"Really? What happened?"

"You're too young to know about these things," said Karen. She didn't think she had the energy to explain everything to Aldo, but seeing the disappointed look on his face, she told him what had happened.

"Do you want me to wait with you?" he offered.

"No, thanks," said Karen. "It's enough of a spectacle for me to stand here."

"OK," Aldo said. "There's a TV program that I want to see at five o'clock, anyhow."

Karen stood at the mailbox and felt sorrier for herself than ever. The mailman came at ten minutes after five. He was a little hard of hearing, and Karen had to explain to him three times why she was standing there.

The mailman nodded his head. "It's happened before, and it will happen again," he said. He wouldn't let Karen touch any of the letters to help him. "It's against federal regulations," he said. Carefully he went through the mail himself.

"Someone's giving a party," he said, when he saw all the green envelopes in a clump.

At last a different shade of green was visible, and

28

the five-dollar bill appeared. The postman looked carefully at Karen. "You've an honest face," he said, handing her the money.

Karen thanked him, and as she walked home she wondered if he had paid her a compliment. "You have an honest face," she told herself.

When Karen entered the house, her mother didn't congratulate her for retrieving the bill. Instead she said, "Where's the milk?"

"What milk?" asked Karen.

"The milk I sent you to buy almost two hours ago."

Karen had to walk back up the street for the third time that afternoon. "I hope it's sour," she muttered to herself, as she carried the milk home. Then she was sorry that she had said that. With her luck, the milk would be sour and her mother would make her return it. She dumped the package on the kitchen counter and sat down exhausted. She was worn out.

On Wednesday, a paper with the name Carin Sossi was returned to Karen. It was the math test that she had taken on Tuesday. More bad luck. She had the second lowest mark in the class. The lowest mark was received by a boy from Korea who had been in the class for only a week and didn't speak any English. In two months, he would probably not only speak English, he would understand the math problems too. Then she would be at the very bottom.

On Thursday, Karen waited in dread. She went from class to class. Everything was quiet. Bad luck didn't strike until lunchtime, when she opened her brown paper lunch bag. She hadn't taken the bag with the baloney sandwich on rye bread and the pear that she had packed for herself the night before. Her bag held a pound of chopped round steak —undoubtedly tonight's supper—wrapped in wax paper.

Since she was a cook herself, Karen thought quickly. She sniffed the meat and it still smelled fine, despite its having been in her school locker for the past three hours instead of inside a refrigerator. She thought of asking one of the cafeteria aides if she might store the meat in their refrigerator, and then she decided that her mother would be concerned if she went looking for it and could only find a baloney sandwich for the family's supper.

So Karen took the bag and went to the school office and asked if she could call home. Twenty minutes later Mrs. Sossi arrived, and the two of them traded brown paper bags. The bad luck had been averted before a crisis but not before Mrs. Sossi had still another reason to think of Karen as the world's most careless child.

"It's just a phase I'm going through," said Karen. "I'll grow out of it."

"But will I survive?" asked Mrs. Sossi.

Then it was Friday. A quiet day. No tests were scheduled at school, so Karen couldn't fail anything. However, she forgot her locker key, which normally would mean a demerit in gym, since she couldn't change her clothing. But the gym teacher made an announcement. "Don't bother changing into shorts today. I'm going to show you a film about basketball." Karen stood speechless. Could her luck be changing?

Good luck would have been a letter or two from her pen pals waiting for her at home, but there weren't any. Good luck would have been her father inviting the whole family to see the new movie in town after supper, but he didn't.

Instead, the phone rang during supper, and Elaine took the call. Eight out of ten phone calls in the Sossi house were for her. The caller was a new woman up the street, Mrs. Collins, and she needed a baby-sitter for the next evening. Elaine said that she was busy. Then she did what Karen had been waiting six months for her to do. She said, "I have a sister who is thirteen. Would you like her to sit for you?"

A moment later Elaine handed over the telephone. Karen's heart beat hard. She could hardly hear the words Mrs. Collins was saying. Imagine! She was finally going to baby-sit and earn money, just like Elaine.

"I'm not sure I would trust you with a baby," Mrs. Sossi said, looking at Karen when she got off the phone. "It's a big responsibility. You can't let your mind wander."

"Don't put the baby in the mailbox," suggested Aldo.

"Wait," said Mr. Sossi. "The best way for Karen to learn responsibility is to give her some responsibility. I'm sure you will do a fine job," he said, smiling at her.

"If you do have any problems, you can call me," Mrs. Sossi suggested.

"There won't be any problems," said Karen.

"There'd better not be any," said Elaine. "After all, I recommended you."

Neither Aldo's teasing nor her mother's doubts could upset Karen. She was feeling too good. As she went upstairs, her mother said, "By the way, I brought your slacks home from the cleaners today."

"Now that I'm going to be earning money I'll be able to pay you back for the trip," said Karen.

She went upstairs and examined her slacks, which were hanging in the front of her closet. The butter stain was gone. That was good luck. Sometimes in the past Karen had succeeded in soiling clothes so badly that the dry cleaners could not remove the mark at all.

She put her hand into the side pocket. She felt something. Slowly she removed a five-dollar bill, ironed flat when the pants had been pressed.

"Look!" she shouted, running down the stairs. "Here's my five-dollar bill. It *was* in the pocket, and it came back with the clean slacks."

"Wow!" said Aldo. "You probably are the only person in all of New Jersey who sends their money out to be cleaned and pressed."

"What good luck!" said Mrs. Sossi.

"Yes," breathed Karen. Perhaps her streak of bad luck really was over.

3.

Hair Conditioning

Karen woke early on Saturday morning, and even before she was fully conscious, she remembered that something good had happened to her. In a minute, it came back to her. She had a baby-sitting job for that evening. Now she was just like Elaine.

Were it not for the family resemblance, the fact that Karen and Elaine were sisters born just eighteen months apart would be hard to believe. Elaine was a good student without having to put in much effort. She remembered things in class, understood math theories, adored French verbs, and handed in neatly written papers on time. She had discovered early in her school career that not only did neatness count, it counted a lot. So Elaine collected her good grades with ease and saved her energy for those things she thought important: her appearance and, more recently, boys.

In the months since they had moved to Woodside, she had established a large clientele of babies who needed supervision on weekend evenings when their parents temporarily abandoned them. Baby-sitting was a lucrative field, and she had invested her earnings in makeup, clothes, and costume jewelry. Mr. Sossi said these things were not a reliable hedge against inflation, but Elaine only replied that her hair looked like a hedge and then spent her next two weeks' earnings on a new haircut.

More than once in recent weeks, Elaine had said to Karen, "Why don't you take better care of yourself? No boy will ever be caught dead looking at you the way you are now. The only thing you have is a good figure. You're lucky that with all the cooking you do, you haven't gotten fat."

"You don't get fat from cooking," said Karen. "Only from eating."

"I know," answered Elaine with a sigh. The

unfortunate result of having a sister who prepared homemade ice cream and butterscotch brownies was already showing on her. Karen nibbled at the finished results of her cooking. She was interested in creating new flavors and textures, but she didn't gorge herself on the finished products. Elaine was the one who ate half a batch of ginger cookies as a midnight snack.

"You should do something about your hair," Elaine told Karen.

"What's wrong with my hair?" Karen wanted to know.

"Well, for one thing, it's all dried out from the sun. You should buy a conditioner and treat your hair properly. If it looks like this now, imagine how it will look when you are twenty."

The last thing on Karen's mind was how her hair might look when she was twenty. At thirteen, she could hardly conceive of ever attaining such an old age. On the other hand, there was a really cute boy named Roy in her science class. Maybe if she looked better, he might notice her.

"It's all right for you to talk," Karen said to Elaine. "You have piles of money to spend on conditioners and things. Maybe when I start earning money, I'll spend some of it on myself too."

But the truth was, Karen doubted that she would ever squander her money on shampoos and such things. Now that she had an ice-cream freezer, she had her eyes on a pasta maker. Imagine making your own spaghetti!

"Well, all I can say is that you look a mess!" said Elaine.

Karen tried to ignore Elaine. There were things much more important than one's appearance. But sometimes, when no one was around, she studied herself in the mirror. Elaine was right about her hair. It was dry and frizzy this fall in a way that it never had been before. During the summer, they had gone swimming almost every day, and except when the lifeguard at the pool reminded her to follow the rules, Karen never wore a swimming cap. She didn't like the way it pressed on her ears. Elaine not only wore a cap in the water, she covered her hair with a scarf when she sat in the sun.

This morning, as she was getting dressed, Karen felt like a new person. After all, she had her first baby-sitting job, which was the beginning of really growing up. She wished that she had a new appearance to go with her new responsibilities. As she combed her hair, she remembered an article that she had seen in one of her mother's magazines.

While flipping the pages from "Soups Made of Leftovers" to an article called "Five-minute Desserts That Taste like Five Hours of Work," her eye had hit on still another article. This one was called "Mayonnaise Magic." Karen already knew one clever recipe in which you mixed mayonnaise with Parmesan cheese to make a canapé that didn't taste like either mayonnaise or cheese. To her disappointment, the article told about the history of mayonnaise and some of its uses other than in cooking. A sentence hit Karen in the eye. "Some people have even used mayonnaise as a conditioner for their hair. The oil content and perhaps the egg yolks too add a glossy quality to hair that is dried and lacking in protein."

All during breakfast Karen thought about the article. She didn't have the money for a bottle of conditioner. (Most of her freshly dry-cleaned five dollar bill was owed to her mother.) But there was a large jar of mayonnaise in the refrigerator at that very moment. Perhaps it would work just as the article said. She put her breakfast dishes in the sink and removed the jar of mayonnaise from the refrigerator. Luckily, no one noticed her walking up the stairs with the jar under her arm. This was an experiment, and she would rather not have anyone know what was happening until it was over and she could produce the results.

She could hear Elaine now, "Oh, Karen, what magnificent luster your hair has! It's so shiny. What brand of conditioner did you use?" She would sound like a woman in a TV commercial.

Karen took the jar into the bathroom and opened it. It smelled like mayonnaise, a fine smell. She loved hard-boiled eggs with a good dollop of mayonnaise mixed with them.

She wished she had thought to bring a spoon upstairs with her. However, the mouth of the jar was large enough so that she could fit her hand inside it. She took a large fistful of the mayonnaise. It had a nice cool, squishy feel to it, and she moved her fingers about within the jar. Then she rubbed her hand through her hair. She had a lot of hair, and so she took still another handful of the mayonnaise. It was like rubbing shampoo into her scalp except that she wasn't getting a lather. Now the next question was, how long should she leave the stuff on her head? Did the article say two hours?

The longer the better, she decided. So she washed her hands, capped the jar, and went into her bedroom. There was a report due for English, and math homework too, but Saturday morning didn't seem like the appropriate time to do either. So Karen took out her box of stationery and decided which of her pen pals she would write to. The smell of mayonnaise disturbed her concentration, though, and her scalp was beginning to itch. She scratched in one spot, and then her fingers were so messy that she had to go back into the bathroom to wash her hands a second time.

"Yikes!" screamed Aldo, as Karen came out of the bathroom. "What happened to you?"

"I've put some conditioner on my hair," said Karen. There was no need to tell him what the conditioner was.

"You smell funny," her brother said. He stood there, looking puzzled. "You smell funny but familiar. I think I've smelled it before."

Karen had no intention of giving away her secret. But before she could escape into her bedroom, Elaine emerged on the scene.

"*Mon dieu!*" she gasped in her ninth-grade French. "Good heavens! What happened to you?"

"Nothing happened," said Karen. "Don't you know hair conditioner when you see it?"

"Hair conditioner? It's a terrible brand. I never saw any that color or that smell."

"Well, you don't know them all," said Karen.

"You told me that my hair needed conditioner, and so I put some on. Now, if you don't mind, I have work to do in my room."

"Macaroni salad," said Elaine. "Why does your conditioner make me think of macaroni salad?"

"It's a little like potato salad too," said Aldo.

"It's very strange," commented Elaine. "When I look at you, I feel a little sick. But if I close my eyes, my mouth starts watering for something to eat."

"Oh, you're always hungry," said Karen, pushing past her sister and into her room.

"Why is there a jar of mayonnaise in the bathroom?" called Aldo.

"Mayonnaise!" shrieked Elaine. "I knew I recognized that smell. Hey, Mom," she called. "Do you know what your crazy daughter did? She made a salad on her head."

Mrs. Sossi came running up the stairs. "What's all the yelling about?" she asked.

"Your daughter has gone bananas," said Elaine, pointing to Karen's room.

"No, she has gone mayonnaise," said Aldo, holding out the jar of salad dressing.

Mrs. Sossi looked puzzled. "What's going on, dear?" she asked. "Do you need any help?"

The strong smell of mayonnaise wafted out of Karen's room. "I'm busy!" she said, pushing the door closed.

"You'd better let me be busy with you," said Mrs. Sossi, pushing the door open and going inside.

In the end, three consecutive shampoos were needed to wash the greasiness and the smell out of Karen's hair. She knew she wouldn't be able to look at egg, tuna, chicken, or potato salad for many weeks without feeling slightly ill. As for her hair, it looked pretty much the same.

"You're lucky," said Elaine. "I would have thought that putting all that mayonnaise on your hair would make it look much, much worse."

Some luck, thought Karen. But she kept her mouth closed. If she weren't looking forward to her first baby-sitting job, she would have been miserable. However, she consoled herself by figuring out how much money she would be earning. Elaine had told Karen to charge $1.00 an hour. Mrs. Collins said that she wanted Karen to come at 6:30 PM. If they went to a movie, they wouldn't be home before 11 PM. If they were going to visit friends, it might be later still. Karen began to count on her fingers: 7:30—8:30—9:30—10:30—11. She could make at least $4.50. Not bad! If the Collins family had her baby-sit for them on a regular basis, she could average $4.50 or $5.00 each weekend. Perhaps sometimes they would go out on both Fridays and Saturdays. Another evening would bring the total up to $9 or $10 a week or $36 to $40 a month. For someone who hated arithmetic, Karen was putting a lot of energy into adding and multiplying, and on a Saturday too.

As she started to figure out how much she could earn over a year, the telephone rang.

"I'll get it," Elaine called. "It's probably for me."

It wasn't. The caller asked to speak to Karen.

"It's a man," said Elaine in a whisper, as she handed the phone to her sister.

Karen wasn't in suspense long. The caller was Mr. Collins, the father of the child she would be sitting for that evening.

"I just want to tell you," he said, "that my wife *thinks* we are going out to dinner. Today's her birthday. Actually, some friends are planning a surprise party back at our house. So I'm just going to take her away for about half an hour."

"Don't you want me to come?" Karen asked, her eyes brimming with tears. She couldn't believe that she was losing her first baby-sitting job.

"Oh, yes," said Mr. Collins. "That's the point.

I want you to come, but I'll have my wife call you to check on things as soon as we reach the restaurant. You tell her that you feel sick; maybe tell her that you threw up," he suggested. "Meanwhile, our friends will arrive at the house, and when we get back, it will be a big surprise."

"Yes," said Karen. "It is a surprise," she added glumly.

"We should be gone for thirty minutes," said Mr. Collins before he hung up.

"What is it?" asked Mrs. Sossi, when Karen put down the phone.

Karen tried to blink back her tears of disappointment as she explained the situation.

"They'll have to pay you for the thirty minutes," said Aldo, trying to console his sister.

Thirty minutes was only fifty cents. No wonder she hated arithmetic, Karen thought. A few minutes ago she had computed an income of hundreds of dollars. But the laws of mathematics didn't take into account human nature and Mrs. Collins' surprise party. Fifty cents! What could you do with fifty cents? Buy a package of graph paper!

Mr. Sossi had walked into the kitchen and heard the end of the discussion. "Karen," he said, putting his arm around her shoulder. "You don't realize it, but you have been hired for something much

46

harder than putting a two-year-old to bed."

"Nothing is harder than putting a two-year-old to bed," said both Elaine and Mrs. Sossi together.

"Karen was hired to be an actress," said Mr. Sossi. "She has to convince Mrs. Collins that she is very ill, even though she will be feeling fine. That's a hard thing to do, but I'm sure she will give an excellent performance, worthy of an Academy Award nomination."

"You could sort of gag while you're talking to her on the telephone," suggested Elaine. She was beginning to feel sorry that she had only a routine baby-sitting job lined up for that evening.

"Tell her that it must be something you had for supper that didn't agree with you," said Aldo.

"No," said Mrs. Sossi. "Mrs. Collins will think I'm a terrible cook. Tell her that you must be coming down with the flu."

Everyone had suggestions for Karen. "It's too bad that you'll have such a small audience for your acting debut," said Mr. Sossi with a laugh. Everyone was laughing now, and even Karen was able to see the humor in the situation. She began to look forward to getting sick. Maybe they would even ask her to baby-sit another time. Though with her luck, she wouldn't count on it, she decided.

4.

Baby-sitting

Supper was finished early that evening, so that both Elaine and Karen would be ready to go off to their baby-sitting jobs. Elaine stood at the door with a notebook and a fat history textbook in her arms. "Even when I don't open my books, they make me look like a serious and reliable person," she explained to Karen.

Karen didn't have any books with her. "I'm only going to be there for half an hour," she said, shrugging her shoulders.

"But Mrs. Collins doesn't know that," said

Aldo. "She thinks you're going to be there all evening."

"You're right," agreed Karen, and she rushed upstairs to grab her math book and some paper.

"These are like stage props," she explained to her mother.

"Good luck," said Mrs. Sossi, as Karen went out the door. Karen started off up the street. She wondered if she should act as if she weren't feeling well from the moment she entered the Collins home. No, that would worry Mrs. Collins, and she wouldn't want to leave her child with Karen. She would have to seem fine at first and then come down with a sudden illness when the phone rang later.

"Hi," said Mrs. Collins, opening the door for Karen. "Keith and I have been waiting for you."

Keith was a little over two years old. He didn't appear to have been waiting for Karen at all. In fact, he took one look at her and began to howl. Perhaps half an hour with Keith would be long enough, thought Karen.

"Hi, Keith," she said brightly. "Do you want to play a game with me?"

"No," howled Keith.

"He's always reluctant to have us go away," Mrs.

Collins said apologetically. "But the minute the door is closed he'll be smiling and happy again. Right, Keith?" she asked him.

"No," howled Keith.

Karen held her arms out to take him. He was really quite heavy.

"No," howled Keith.

Mr. Collins came downstairs. "We won't be home late," he said. "We're having dinner in the new Italian restaurant in town. We should be back by nine thirty or ten o'clock."

Karen wondered if the party had been called off. But just then Mr. Collins winked at her. Karen guessed the plans were still the same as he had explained them to her on the telephone that afternoon.

Mrs. Collins showed Karen where the phone number for the pediatrician, the fire department, the police department, Keith's grandparents, and two reliable neighbors were listed. "These should cover all emergencies," she said.

Karen nodded, knowing that she was not likely to need any of the numbers during such a short evening.

"No," howled Keith. Karen wondered if he could say anything else.

51

"Good night, Keith," said Mr. Collins, and he kissed his son.

"Good night, Keith," said Mrs. Collins. "Karen is going to put you into your crib now, and you'll get a good sleep. When you wake up in the morning, Mommy and Daddy will be right here."

"No," howled Keith.

The door closed. Karen looked around the house. Keith struggled to get out of her arms. "Here," said Karen, walking into the kitchen. "Is this your bedroom?"

"No," howled Keith.

Karen held tightly to the squirming child. She opened a door in the kitchen. It was a broom closet. "Is this your bedroom?"

"No," howled Keith.

She opened another door. It was a bathroom. "Oh. Is this your bedroom?"

"No," said Keith, but he didn't cry. He looked at Karen. "Batroom," he said.

Karen walked toward the stairs. "We have to find your bedroom," she said. She put Keith down. "Let's look upstairs," she said. To her relief, he began to crawl up the stairs. She didn't think she had the energy to carry him all the way up.

At the top of the stairs, there was a large bedroom with a double bed. "Is this your bedroom?" she asked.

"No," said Keith. He laughed. He liked the game that they were playing.

Karen opened two more doors. One was a linen closet, and another was a bathroom. Keith laughed and laughed. Finally they came to his room. She had just put Keith into his crib when the telephone rang. She couldn't believe that half an hour had passed so quickly.

"I've got to answer the phone," she said to Keith.

"No," he howled.

She didn't want him to cry again. "Come," said Karen. "Show me where the telephone is."

She helped Keith climb out of the crib as the phone rang a second time.

"Here," said Keith, opening the door of his closet.

"No," said Karen. The phone rang a third time.

"Here," said Keith, rushing to the bathroom.

"No," howled Karen.

The phone rang a fourth time. She was sure the telephone was in the master bedroom, but she couldn't leave Keith alone. That was the first rule of baby-sitting, Elaine had told her. Never leave the child alone unless he is in bed or old enough to take care of himself.

The phone rang a fifth time.

Karen scooped Keith up and ran to the bedroom. There was a phone beside the bed. She answered it breathlessly. "Hello," she said.

"Hi, Karen," said the voice at the other end. "How are you making out with baby-sitting?"

For a moment, Karen couldn't place the voice. "Aldo," she shrieked. "What are you calling me for? I'm too busy to talk on the telephone to you."

"I just wanted to know how it was going," Aldo said.

"Terrible," said Karen, and she hung up.

She picked Keith up and carried him back to his bedroom.

The phone rang again. "Oh, no," said Karen.

Holding on to Keith, she rushed back to the phone. This time it would certainly be Mrs. Collins. She made her voice sound weak and helpless and said softly into the telephone, "Hello." She hoped she sounded as if she were dying.

"Karen, are you all right?" asked an anxious voice at the other end. It wasn't Mrs. Collins. It was Mrs. Sossi.

"Mom, how can I do any baby-sitting if the whole family keeps calling me here?" complained Karen.

"Aldo said that you told him things were terrible."

"They are only terrible when I have to stop baby-sitting and speak to you on the telephone," said Karen. "I don't remember you calling Elaine every three minutes when she goes baby-sitting." Karen banged the receiver down on the phone.

She picked up Keith and carried him back to his crib. Keith sat up in his bed, grinning. "Phone," he said. Karen listened, but the phone was not ring-ing. "No more," she said. "No more phone calls." As she spoke, the telephone rang again.

By now she was really getting angry. She picked up Keith once again and rushed to the bedroom where the phone was ringing.

"I told you to stop calling me," she said into the receiver.

"Karen? What's the matter? Are you all right?" The voice wasn't her mother's, nor was it Aldo's or her father's. This time it really was Mrs. Collins.

"Oh," said Karen, feeling flustered. "I'm fine, it's just that I thought you were someone else. Everything's fine here." She stopped for a moment and realized what she had said. "I mean, every-thing isn't fine. I feel sick. In fact, that's why I thought you were my mother calling. I called her to say that I thought I was going to throw up. I feel awful. I don't know what it is. I may be coming down with a contagious disease. I think you had better come home," said Karen, the words spilling out of her mouth as fast as she could think of them.

"That's awful," said Mrs. Collins. "Keep away from Keith. I'll be there as fast as I can."

Karen put down the phone. "Oh, Keith," she said to the little boy. "I almost messed that up!" She giggled.

The downstairs bell was ringing. She couldn't believe that Mr. and Mrs. Collins had returned home so quickly.

Karen went downstairs and peeked through the window of the living room. An elderly woman was on the porch, and she was holding an enormous cake box. She didn't look the least bit like a robber, and so Karen decided it was safe to open the door.

"I'm Keith's grandmother," she introduced herself. "Everyone else is hiding out in the back. They've parked their cars a block or two away. Let's open the back door for them so that they have time to hide before my daughter and son-in-law return."

Keith was running about with delight. Karen thought this evening must be the strangest he'd ever had with a baby-sitter. They went to the kitchen and opened the back door. There were about twenty people standing there, all holding gift-wrapped packages. Quickly they filed into the house and hid behind the sofa and chairs in the living room.

Karen heard a car drive up in front of the house. "I think they're home," she said.

Sure enough, she heard a key in the door, and Mr. and Mrs. Collins entered. "Karen! We're back," Mrs. Collins shouted. When she saw Keith standing next to his baby-sitter, she said, "Keith, don't stand near Karen. She's sick!"

"No," said Keith. He didn't seem at all pleased to see his parents again so soon. He had been having too much fun without them.

Suddenly all the hidden people jumped out from behind the chairs and sofa and shouted, "Surprise!"

Mrs. Collins let out a shriek.

"Happy birthday, dear," Mr. Collins said to his wife. "You are a quarter of a century old."

Mrs. Collins looked around at all her friends and at her son, who was trying to open one of the fancy gift-wrapped boxes on the floor, and she also looked at her new baby-sitter.

"I feel as if I'm a hundred," she gasped. "Karen, do you mean to say that you aren't sick at all?"

Karen grinned. "Happy birthday, Mrs. Collins," she said.

Karen had expected to be paid fifty cents and sent home. Instead, Mr. Collins asked if she would be able to stay and help serve. So she helped Keith's grandmother set the table and put out the food for the guests. Except for the cake that she had brought in with her, all of the rest of the food was in cars parked two blocks away. There were two hero sandwiches, each six feet long, and containers of pickles, potato salad, and cole slaw. Karen wrinkled her nose with distaste as she smelled the mayonnaise. She had seen and smelled enough of it already for one day.

What a day this had been and what an evening too! She had worked as a baby-sitter, an actress, and also a waitress. She couldn't wait to tell her family about her experiences, although she was a little ashamed about the way she had shouted at them on the telephone.

When the time came to walk her home, Mr. Collins gave her ten dollars. "This is higher than the usual rate," he said, "but this wasn't the usual job."

"Karen," said Mrs. Collins, "now that you are feeling well again, I hope you will be able to sit for us often. Keith really seems to like you. And besides, I've been cheated out of a dinner at the new Italian restaurant, even though I had a lovely party instead."

"Do you think you could sit for us a week from tonight?" asked Mr. Collins.

"Sure," said Karen happily. "I'd love to." She wasn't acting at all. She really meant it.

5.

John Dark and Other Homework

Homework was a pain, Karen thought. No matter what she was doing these days, in the back of her mind there was always the nagging reminder of undone homework. She had to write a weekly composition for English, and she had to come up with an idea for a science project that would be due in December. Both subjects bored her to tears. She wished she didn't have to go to school and could just stay home and do the things she wanted.

The funny thing, though, was that what she most enjoyed doing was *real* homework. She loved

61

experimenting in the kitchen with a new recipe. Elaine, who was very good at school subjects, hated to spend any time in the kitchen unless she was eating there.

So, although she should have been doing homework for school, Karen spent several hours each weekend in the kitchen, cooking or baking something new. Today she was making two loaves of whole-wheat bread. She had never baked bread before, but it turned out to be quite simple and a lot of fun. Working with yeast was not nearly as difficult as she had anticipated. Making the dough and punching it into shape was fun.

Elaine stuck her head into the kitchen and asked, "Who are you pretending that you're hitting?"

"My math teacher. She's a witch," said Karen, but at that moment she really didn't mean it. She was enjoying herself too much to worry about her math teacher or her science teacher or her English teacher.

"Just be sure that you clean up any mess that you make," Mrs. Sossi said. She always said the same thing. Karen was pretty good about cleaning up, and sometimes if Aldo and his friend DeDe were around, she could bribe them with some of her finished goods to help her with the cleanup.

Finally the bread dough was set in a bowl to rise. Walking out of the kitchen, Karen saw her father was watching a football game in the living room. Mrs. Sossi was nowhere to be seen. Karen suspected that she had gone to another garage sale in town. Her mother spent many Sunday afternoons that way; she was always hunting for bargains.

Karen went upstairs and saw Aldo through the open door of his room. He was moping on his bed. "What's up?" she asked him.

"I just remembered that I have to give a report on John Dark tomorrow, and I forgot to go to the library."

"You should plan ahead," said Karen, quoting her mother. How many times a week did she hear those words? "Anyhow, who is John Dark?"

"He's a famous person. Everyone in my class picked a different person to do a report on," said Aldo.

"I never heard of him," said Karen, shrugging her shoulders. "He can't be that famous."

"I know. He isn't even in the encyclopedia. I looked." Aldo sighed.

"It's not the most up-to-date set," Karen agreed, referring to the encyclopedia published in 1962 that her mother had recently bought at a garage sale.

"Maybe you didn't do it right," she suggested hopefully. "I'll help you."

The two of them went to the hallway bookshelf that held the set of books. They had only cost ten dollars, so they were a real bargain, except that everything Karen or Elaine or Aldo wanted to look up seemed to have happened after 1962. Probably John Dark had become famous since then too. Karen wondered if he was an astronaut.

She turned to the *D* volume, but there was nothing there. "See," said Aldo. "I told you there wasn't anything."

"What do you know about John Dark?" asked Karen.

"Nothing."

"Don't you have any idea why he is famous? Was he a scientist?"

"I don't know," said Aldo.

"Did he invent something?"

"I don't know."

"Do you think he was in politics?" asked Karen.

"I don't know."

"Well, why did you pick his name?" asked Karen.

"I don't know," said Aldo helplessly. "The teacher called out a bunch of names, and each of us chose one to do a report on. When she said John Dark, I raised my hand. I guess I should have picked Louis the Fourteenth."

"Louis the Fourteenth?" said Karen. "What other names were there?"

"Marie Antoinette. That's who DeDe picked. And other famous people from French history."

"French history," said Karen. "I bet Elaine would know!"

Elaine was just getting ready to leave the house. "Did you ever hear of a man named John Dark?" asked Karen.

"Nope," said Elaine, zipping her jacket.

"Aldo says John Dark was important in French history," said Karen. "I thought you knew everything about France and things French."

Elaine thought a moment. "John Dark," she said. "Jeanne d'Arc! Of course I've heard of *her*. That's the French way of saying Joan of Arc. Boy, you really are stupid if you thought she was a man!" she said, as she slammed the door behind her.

Karen was so pleased that the mystery of John Dark was solved that she wasn't offended by Elaine's words. She rushed back to Aldo, who was thumbing his way through the pages of the *D* volume of the encyclopedia. "It's Jeanne d'Arc," she said. "You volunteered to write about Jeanne d'Arc."

"That's what I said," said Aldo. "John Dark."

Karen reached for the *A* volume. Since she didn't have a last name, the French heroine was probably listed under Arc. She turned the pages without success.

"This encyclopedia is no good," complained Aldo.

"Wait," said Karen. "Let me look under *J.*"

"I learned that people are always under their last names in the encyclopedia," said Aldo.

"I know," said Karen. "I learned that too. But sometimes teachers are wrong," she said hopefully. Sure enough, there in the *J* volume was a long article about Joan of Arc. "Look," she said triumphantly, pointing to a picture. "That's Jeanne d'Arc."

"You mean John Dark is a woman!" Aldo gasped, gaping at the drawing in the book in front of him. "That's how he spells his name?" he asked.

"Sure," said Karen. "In French, Jeanne d'Arc is pronounced like John Dark. And she was very famous. Even I've heard of her."

"Now I really am in trouble," said Aldo.

"What's the problem?" asked Karen. "Boys can write reports on women. It's no big deal."

"That's what you think," said Aldo. "We're supposed to dress up like our historical figure and tell about his life. How can I dress up like a lady?"

Karen started laughing. "What did your teacher say when you picked Jeanne d'Arc?" she asked.

"She just said, 'That will be interesting to see.' But I didn't know what she meant."

"Ohhhhhh, wait! I forgot my bread," said Karen, and she rushed off to the kitchen. Anxiously she checked the large bowl filled with dough. Sure enough, just as the instructions said, the dough had increased in quantity during the time she had been spending with Aldo. She punched it some more and once again covered it with a damp towel.

"It sure doesn't look like bread," said Aldo. "Maybe you did something wrong."

"Be patient," said Karen.

They left the kitchen and began discussing Jeanne d'Arc. Aldo phoned his friend DeDe for suggestions. "Stop laughing," he scolded her over the phone.

"She's going to make a fake head and pretend that she got her head cut off, because that really happened to Marie Antoinette," he told Karen, after he hung up. "I wish I could do something neat like that."

"There must be something you can do too," Karen consoled Aldo. "Just don't set your class-room on fire!" She thought some more and turned to look at the pages about Jeanne d'Arc in the encyclopedia again.

"Let me go and put the bread into the oven, and then I'll tell you what to do," said Karen. "I think I have an idea."

Karen returned from the kitchen carrying a roll of aluminum foil. "Here," she said. "We can use this. Bring me a wire clothes hanger, an old sheet, a candlestick with a candle, and a baseball bat."

"You sound like Cinderella's fairy godmother," said Aldo, puzzled over this peculiar list of objects. "Next you'll want me to bring you two white rats. I think you'd better stick to making bread."

"No, no," said Karen. "It will work. You'll see."

Aldo ran about the house getting the needed supplies.

"I thought of something else," said Karen, when he had assembled all the things on the floor of his room. "Get your woolen ski hat. The one that Grandma knit you last winter and you never want to wear."

Aldo dug into his bottom drawer and found the hat. "It itches," he complained. "I don't like it."

"That's OK. It's perfect for the purpose," said Karen. "Look." She pointed to the picture of Jeanne d'Arc in the encyclopedia. "That ski hat is just like the helmet that she wore. Now when it's time for your report, turn off the lights in the classroom and light a candle for atmosphere. Then put the sheet around you and the ski cap on your head, and you can say that you are the ghost of Jeanne d'Arc."

"What about the baseball bat?" asked Aldo.

"Cover that with aluminum foil, and it will be your sword."

"Hey, that's great," said Aldo. "In the dark, I won't mind being a woman so much either."

"Besides, if you read about her, you'll see that she was very brave and special. And you know, she even became a saint."

"What's the hanger for?" asked Aldo. "To hang up the sheet after I use it?"

"No, no," said Karen. "Here," she said, picking it up. "If you pull it out of shape and wrap it with foil, you can make it into a halo. Then, just before you finish your talk, you can hold it over your head by the hook and explain that you have been made into a saint."

69

"That's fantastic," said Aldo. "Thanks for helping me. I know I'll get a good mark now."

Karen glanced at her wristwatch. "Let's go check the bread. It should be ready by this time."

The odor of the baking bread filled the house. The smell was wonderful. Considering that the house had been so quiet before, the kitchen was suddenly filled. Elaine, who had been in such a hurry to rush off before, had reappeared on the scene. It was half time at the football game, and Mr. Sossi came into the kitchen looking for a snack. Mrs. Sossi was sitting in the kitchen going through the contents of a paper shopping bag and eager to show off her purchases. "Look," she said proudly, holding up a small dish. "This is a Wedgwood ashtray, and it cost only twenty-five cents." Since none of them smoked, none of them was properly impressed.

No one looked at Mrs. Sossi. Everyone was looking at Karen's bread. Even the family cats, Peabody and Poughkeepsie, had come into the kitchen, and they didn't even eat bread. The two brown loaves looked wonderful, but they smelled even better.

"We have to let them cool," said Karen.

"I can't wait," said Elaine, taking the butter out of the refrigerator. Aldo reached for the jar of

peanut butter in the cupboard, and Mr. Sossi took out a jar of apricot jam. Mrs. Sossi got some cream cheese. When they all had their own favorite spread ready, they refused to wait any longer.

Karen took a knife and began slicing into one of the loaves. She knew she should wait a little longer until it had cooled, but she was just as eager as the rest of her family to see how the bread had turned out.

"It sure looks like real bread," said Aldo.

"But how does it taste?" asked Karen.

The replies weren't very clear, because everyone had a mouthful of food. But heads went up and down in agreement. Hands went out for seconds.

"Karen," said Aldo, when his mouth was empty enough to speak, "you're a genius! First John Dark and now this. You're great!"

Karen thought of the report card she would be getting one of these days. It wouldn't be the card of a genius.

"John Dark? Who is John Dark?" asked Mrs. Sossi.

"He's an important woman that I have to do a report on, and Karen helped me. I bet I get an A because of Karen," said Aldo happily. He reached for another slice of bread.

"Karen has the perfect fifth-grade mind," said

Elaine. "Too bad she's in eighth grade."

Karen stuck her tongue out at Elaine and pulled the second loaf of bread away from her before she could cut into it. She wrapped it in the piece of aluminum foil that Aldo had left after making his sword and halo. The bread would make good sandwiches for lunch tomorrow.

6.

A
Halloween
Party

Halloween was on Friday this year. Mrs. Sossi stocked up on miniature candy bars, which she hid away so they wouldn't be consumed before the local children came trick-or-treating. Elaine's friend Sandy was giving a party, and the two older girls spent a lot of time together giggling over the costumes and games they were planning. Aldo was going out trick-or-treating with DeDe and a couple of other friends.

"This is your lucky year, Mom," he said, when they were talking about the approaching holiday.

"You won't have to fix up any costume for me."

"Aren't you going to dress up?" she asked, surprised.

"Sure I am," said Aldo. "But I already have a great costume."

"What is it?" asked Elaine.

"I'm going to wear my John Dark outfit. It got me an A at school, and it's perfect for Halloween too."

"It *is* original," agreed Mrs. Sossi.

"Original!" said Elaine. "He's probably the first and only boy in the history of the world to dress up as Jeanne d'Arc."

Aldo grinned happily. He was pleased with his plan and no longer the least bit self-conscious about playing the role of a woman.

The only one without plans was Karen. She kept hoping that Mrs. Collins would phone and ask her to baby-sit. She was too old to go trick-or-treating, and she didn't have anything special to do for Halloween. Now and then she wondered what the others in her class were doing, but she would never dream of asking anyone. Probably they were all going to parties to which she had not been invited. She would be glad when Halloween was over.

Three days before Halloween, Karen came home

from school with a party invitation. "I can't believe it," she said, shaking her head in disbelief. "Whoever heard of such a thing?"

Mrs. Sossi looked over Karen's shoulder at the page she was reading. It was a message from Mrs. Nesbitt, her math teacher, inviting all her students to her house for Halloween evening.

"Isn't that lovely!" said Mrs. Sossi. "She lives right here in town, and I guess she wanted to give you all something safe and pleasant to do for the evening."

"*Pleasant?*" said Karen. "Spending the evening with your math teacher? A Friday evening? Never. I'm staying home."

"Don't be silly," said her mother. "Your friends from school will all be there. It will be a wonderful opportunity for you to socialize with them."

Karen cringed. Didn't her mother realize that she didn't have any real *friends* at school? Of course she knew all her classmates by name, and they nodded to her on the street, but she couldn't call them friends.

"I'd rather stay home," said Karen. "It's bad enough seeing my math teacher five days a week. I'm not going to spend a Friday evening with her too."

"Look," said Mrs. Sossi, ignoring Karen's words, "it says costumes encouraged. I could help you fix something to wear."

"I said I wasn't going, and that's that!" said Karen. She thought the subject was closed, but her mother didn't.

"Are your classmates wearing costumes to Mrs. Nesbitt's party?" she asked Karen the next day.

"I don't know. I doubt that any of them are going," said Karen.

"Why ever not?" asked Mrs. Sossi.

"I told you that no one in their right mind would spend a Friday evening with their math teacher," said Karen. It was incredible how dense parents could be.

"Well, in that case, there's all the more reason for you to go. Imagine if you gave a party and no one came, how badly you would feel. You must be polite and go. It's the least that you can do."

Karen didn't tell her mother that the very reason she would never even consider giving a party was that she was sure no one would come. It would serve Mrs. Nesbitt right if she were so foolish. If you know that no one would want to come to your party, then you shouldn't even attempt to give one.

At school, Karen listened as her classmates spoke to one another. No one said anything about going

78

to Mrs. Nesbitt's party. Finally she got up her courage and asked Annette Rubin, the girl who sat next to her in math, about it. "Are you going to Mrs. Nesbitt's Halloween party?"

Annette crossed her eyes for a moment. "Do you think I'm crazy?" she asked.

"No," said Karen. "But I was just checking."

"I will be the only one there," Karen said again, when her mother raised the subject on Friday.

"Karen, I am asking this as a personal favor. I want you to go to the party. You are not such a good student that you can afford to insult your math teacher. At least, show her that you have good manners, even if you can't always complete the homework that she assigns."

Karen watched as Aldo put on the sheet and the woolen ski cap. He had his foil-covered baseball-bat-sword in one hand and a shopping bag in the other.

"Jeanne d'Arc wouldn't have been caught dead with a shopping bag," said Elaine, coming down the stairs.

"Who knows?" said Mr. Sossi. "Perhaps a shopping bag might have changed the course of history."

"I need it for my loot," said Aldo, as he marched out the door.

Karen looked at Elaine, who was dressed as a cross between a Gypsy and a ballet dancer and goodness knows what else. "What are you supposed to be?" she asked. Elaine was clothed in a black leotard, short skirt, and moth-eaten fur collar. She was also wearing a great deal of costume jewelry and makeup.

"I'm a high-fashion model," said Elaine, tossing her head.

The doorbell rang just as Elaine was about to leave. Two little girls or two little boys in Mickey Mouse costumes stood there. Karen wished that she were six years old again. She put a candy bar in each of the outstretched hands and shut the door.

"Karen, I'm ready to drive you over to Mrs. Nesbitt's," said her mother. "Your father will stay here and answer the doorbell for the little kids." She handed a foil-wrapped package to Karen. "This is one of the carrot cakes that you made last month. I took it out of the freezer this morning to thaw. I'm sure that Mrs. Nesbitt will be glad of extra food with so many kids coming to her house."

Karen didn't know why she got into the car. She didn't know why she was giving in. She felt limp and defeated. Until her mother had reminded her of her poor math grade, she had not even remotely considered attending the party. At least, no one would know that she had gone. She would stay a little while and then leave, and she would never tell a soul that she had gone. Imagine being the only one to attend a party.

At the door of Mrs. Nesbitt's house, Mrs. Sossi stopped the car. "Would you like me to go in with you and meet your teacher?" she asked.

"This isn't Parents Visiting Night at school," said Karen crossly. "I'll be home soon. Very soon." Like fifteen minutes, she promised herself.

She got out of the car and rang the doorbell.

Mrs. Nesbitt opened the door. To Karen's amazement, her teacher was wearing a costume. She was dressed as a witch. Imagine being a witch and having the nerve to dress up as one too. She couldn't believe it.

"Hello, Karen," said Mrs. Nesbitt, inviting her inside. "You are the very first."

Suddenly Karen felt a stab of compassion for her teacher. She was glad that she had come. Mrs. Nesbitt obviously enjoyed Halloween, and she was going to be very disappointed when no one else arrived at her party.

"I brought this cake that I made," said Karen. "It's a carrot cake."

"You made it yourself?" asked Mrs. Nesbitt,

unwrapping the cake and putting it out on a large table that was loaded with platters of doughnuts and gallon jugs of cider.

"Help yourself to doughnuts," said her teacher. "I was worried that I hadn't bought enough. I know your cake will be consumed before the evening is out. I think I'll take a piece now before it's all gone."

Karen looked around the empty room. She looked back at the crowded table. She hadn't eaten much supper. Thoughts of this party had really killed her appetite, so perhaps now she would be able to help out and eat two, or even three, doughnuts. Who was going to eat all the rest? Mrs. Nesbitt was going to be eating doughnuts from now until Christmas, she decided.

"Oh, Karen, this is delicious," said Mrs. Nesbitt. "Where did you learn how to make it?"

Before Karen could answer, the doorbell rang. Karen had an idea. She would suggest to Mrs. Nesbitt that she give out doughnuts to the little children who came trick-or-treating. If she didn't have four dozen doughnuts sitting on the table at the end of the evening, she would be better able to pretend that her party had been a success, even if no one attended it but one failing math student.

Mrs. Nesbitt opened the door. There were three figures, all in costumes. "Come in, come in, whoever you are," cried Mrs. Nesbitt.

The figures entered. They were dressed as scarecrows in old patched clothing and with bits of straw coming out of their sleeves. "Hi, Mrs. Nesbitt," said one of them.

Karen recognized the voice and froze. It was Roy Nevins from her class at school. She had heard Roy say that no way would he attend his math teacher's party. The bell rang again before Karen could discover who the other scarecrows were. Mrs. Nesbitt opened the door. A ghost entered wearing a sheet that dragged to the floor.

The door was hardly closed before the bell rang again. Karen stood in a corner feeling both stunned and self-conscious. She was amazed that all her classmates seemed to be coming to this party despite their protests to the contrary. Perhaps their mothers had forced them, just as hers had. The room was filling up with guests, and everyone but Karen was in a costume. One girl was wearing her older sister's high-school cheerleader outfit. One boy was wearing his father's old army jacket and cap.

The ghost approached Karen. "I know I said I

wasn't coming," said a voice from under the sheet, "but my mother said I had to." Karen recognized the voice. It was Annette Rubin.

"My mother said I had to come too," said Karen. "I wish she had said I had to wear a costume."

"I have an idea," said Annette. "Wait a minute." She went over to Mrs. Nesbitt and whispered something in her ear. The teacher left the room and returned with a pair of scissors, which she gave Annette.

"Look," said Annette to Karen. "This sheet is enormous. It's king-size. It was the only white one my mother had, and she was furious because I cut holes in it for eyes. Well, she can't get any madder than she already is, so let's cut two more eyeholes, and we can be Siamese twin ghosts under the same sheet."

She measured where to cut. "Stand still," she told Karen. "Look," said Annette with a giggle. She had pulled the sheet over Karen and herself. There was a large mirror in the room, and when they looked in it, four eyes stared out at them from under the sheet.

Annette took Karen's hand. "It will be hard walking around, so we'll have to sit together," she said.

Karen nodded her head under the sheet.

The doorbell kept ringing. In addition to her classmates, many other people were coming too. Apparently this party was an old tradition with Mrs. Nesbitt. Former students returned year after year.

Everyone stood around eating doughnuts and drinking cider. When Annette and Karen walked over to the refreshment table together, Karen could see that her carrot cake had already disappeared. In order to eat, Annette and Karen had to take the sheet off their heads. They put it over their shoulders and stood side by side. Karen took a jelly doughnut and, with her first bite, a blob of red jam squirted out of the far end of the doughnut and landed on the white sheet.

"Oh, I'm sorry!" said Karen.

"Your partner is a slob," commented Roy Nevins, looking at the jam on the white sheet.

"Who cares?" said Annette. "A bloody ghost is even better than a Siamese-twin ghost." She giggled.

"Did you really make that carrot cake?" Roy asked Karen.

She nodded, blushing.

"I like the way you cook vegetables," he said. "You could give my mother a few lessons." He

stuffed a doughnut in his mouth and walked away.

After a while, Karen and Annette removed the sheet so that they could move about more easily. However, they still stayed near each other and talked together.

Mrs. Nesbitt had a deck of tarot cards, and she told everyone's fortune. To Karen, she said, "You have a little trouble with numbers." Karen blushed. She knew just which numbers the fortune-teller meant. But then Mrs. Nesbitt continued. "However, when it comes to really important numbers like three quarters of a teaspoon or one half a tablespoon, you have an excellent ability."

Karen didn't call home to say she was ready to be picked up till the very end of the party. She and Annette helped wash up the dishes and gather the paper cups for the garbage. There wasn't a single doughnut left.

"It was a lovely party," she remembered to say, as she told her math teacher good-bye.

"I love Halloween," Mrs. Nesbitt said. "Thank you for coming and for your wonderful carrot cake. I was smart to take that first slice so quickly. It was gone before I could turn around."

"How was the party?" asked her father, as Karen got into the car.

"OK," said Karen, knowing full well that it was much better than OK. She was awfully glad that she had gone, but she certainly wasn't going to tell her parents so.

Some things one kept to oneself, she thought. She smiled in the dark as she remembered the sheet with the four eyeholes and the plate empty of carrot cake and Roy Nevins dressed as a scarecrow.

7.

Sneezes and Tears

After the Halloween party, Karen hoped that Annette would suggest that they get together after school one day. Karen missed having a best friend. She sat with a few girls at lunchtime every day, and others nodded to her in the school hallways or out in the street, but she couldn't call anyone her special friend. Most of the time she was able to convince herself that she didn't care much. She kept busy at home with her cooking and her letter writing. Sometimes she went to a movie with Aldo on the weekend. Sometimes, but not very often, Elaine let her tag along if she was going roller skating with Sandy. Elaine was lucky. She had found a friend right on their new street within two days of moving to Woodside.

In the past few weeks, much of Karen's time had also been occupied with baby-sitting. Some afternoons when she came home from school, Mrs. Collins would phone and ask her to come and stay with Keith while she went shopping or to the dentist. Being in charge of Keith was fun, but she still would have enjoyed having a friend her own age.

Now maybe Annette would be that friend. Karen managed to walk next to Annette as they moved from one classroom to another down the school corridors, but Annette didn't say much. At lunchtime, they sat at the same table, but Annette seemed preoccupied. She wasn't unfriendly, but she wasn't exactly friendly either. Karen began to think that she must have dreamed sharing the sheet with her classmate on Halloween. Annette hardly seemed the same person who had giggled with her at Mrs. Nesbitt's party.

Finally, after thinking about it for several days, Karen decided that she would take the first step herself. Perhaps Annette was shy.

"Could you come to my house after school tomorrow?" she asked Annette hesitantly, as they walked out of the math class. Suppose Annette wasn't shy at all and just didn't want to come to her house?

"I can't," said Annette. "I have a piano lesson."

The reason seemed like a good one, a real one that hadn't been suddenly invented to avoid visiting. Karen took a deep breath and tried again.

"How about on Wednesday?" she asked.

"I don't think I can," Annette told her. "My piano teacher is holding a recital this Friday evening, and I have to practice every day. I'm going to be a concert pianist when I grow up," she announced.

"Really?" Karen was impressed. She had never known anyone who was going to be a professional musician.

"I've been taking lessons ever since I was four years old," Annette explained. "I practice every day for two or three hours. It keeps me very busy, but if I want to be a pianist, that's what I have to do."

"Wow," said Karen. No wonder Annette didn't have time for friendships.

But then Annette smiled and said, "I have an idea, though. Could I come to your house on Saturday? I could practice in the morning, and then I'd be free in the afternoon."

"Sure," said Karen. She felt like skipping down

the hallway, even though she was on her way to social studies.

By the time Saturday arrived, Karen had baked two batches of cookies in preparation for her guest. She made chocolate chip and oatmeal, and she hid them from Elaine and Aldo. They could have whatever was left over.

Annette arrived after lunch. Karen was at the door waiting for her. This afternoon was the first time she had invited a classmate home since they moved to Woodside.

"Hi," she greeted Annette. "I'm glad you could come." She took her friend around and introduced her to Mrs. Sossi and Aldo. Karen's mother was buttoning up her raincoat. She was about to take Aldo to the dentist. Elaine was not around, and Karen was just as glad.

"Would you like to see my room?" Karen asked Annette. Annette nodded, and Karen led the way.

"I wish we had a piano so you could show me how you play. I bet you're great," said Karen, beaming at her.

Annette nodded in agreement. She stifled a sneeze as she walked into Karen's room. "This is a nice room," she said. "I have to share my bedroom with my little sister."

"I used to share a room when we lived in the city," said Karen. "It's nice having my own room and some privacy at last. There should be a law against older sisters."

Too late she realized that Annette was an older sister.

Annette sneezed again. "Oh, dear, do you have any tissues?" Annette asked Karen.

"Here," said Karen, handing a box to Annette. "Do you think you're getting a cold?" she asked.

"I don't know," said Annette. "I felt fine ten minutes ago." She began wiping tears from her eyes.

Karen wondered if she had hurt Annette's feelings when she said how awful big sisters were. "I bet you're a nicer big sister than Elaine is," Karen said, attempting to make amends. "When is your birthday?"

"It's June twelfth," said Annette.

"Mine is September first," said Karen. "So you're older than me, but not old enough to be my big sister."

"If I was old enough to be your big sister, then I couldn't be in your class at school," Annette pointed out.

Annette blew her nose and wiped some more tears from her eyes.

"You're right," agreed Karen. "I'm awfully glad that you're in my class." She paused for a moment and then leaned over and half whispered to Annette. "What do you think of Roy Nevins?"

Annette shrugged her shoulders. "He's OK, I guess," she said. "I think Peter London looks a little like Robert Redford. Don't you?"

"I never noticed," said Karen. "But I'll take a good look at him on Monday and let you know."

Annette wiped her eyes again. "Is everything all right?" asked Karen.

"Everything's fine," said Annette, smiling through her tears. "I'm allergic to dust," she said. "I think that must be what is bothering me."

"This house is very clean," said Karen defensively. "We just vacuumed this morning. In fact, I was probably vacuuming my room while you were playing the piano."

Annette shrugged her shoulders.

"Would you like some milk and cookies?" Karen asked. Perhaps another location might have a better effect on Annette and her nose and eyes. "I made the cookies myself," she said.

Karen was relieved that none of her family was in the kitchen. She was a little embarrassed to have a brand-new friend sitting in the kitchen and crying.

"These are very good," said Annette, biting into a second oatmeal cookie. Even if she was enjoying the cookies, however, Annette still kept on crying.

"Listen, Annette," Karen said. "I really would like to be your friend. If something is bothering you, I wish you would tell me. Did I say something to insult you? I didn't mean it about outlawing older sisters. It's just that my older sister is so mean to me sometimes. I'm sure you aren't like that with your little sister."

"Well, little sisters can be pretty dreadful too,"

said Annette, blowing her nose. "But you can't be as bad as my little sister. In the first place, you aren't seven years old. And in the second place, I bet you wouldn't jump all over the house with your friends and make a lot of noise when I was practicing. It's very hard to concentrate when my sister is around."

"Do you really practice three hours every day?" asked Karen.

Annette nodded her head and wiped away a few new tears. "Sometimes I get up early and practice for an hour before I go to school," she said.

"Gosh," said Karen, overcome with awe. "I can hardly get out of bed in the morning. It sure must take a lot of willpower to get up so early."

"Concert pianists need a lot of self-discipline," said Annette.

"How was your recital?" asked Karen. Maybe Annette was upset because she had made a lot of mistakes and couldn't become a concert pianist after all.

"It was wonderful! I really felt I played very well. And everyone said so too," said Annette. But she wiped away more tears as she spoke.

Karen began to wish that Elaine was home. Her older sister might be a pain most of the time, but at least if she were here she would be able to keep the conversation going. She was lively and friendly, and none of her friends ever broke into tears the moment they entered the house. Something was obviously upsetting Annette, and Karen didn't know what it was or what to do about it.

Just then Peabody walked into the kitchen. The cats had developed a new life-style since moving to New Jersey. They had discovered a broken window in the basement, which enabled them to enter or leave the house whenever they wanted. For two animals who had never seen the outdoors before, they had become remarkably independent.

"Oh, you have a cat," said Annette, looking down at Peabody.

"We have two cats. This is Peabody. The other one is named Poughkeepsie. He's probably around somewhere. You'll see him before you go home."

"I guess that's why I'm sneezing and everything," said Annette. "I'm allergic to cats. Even when they aren't in the house, their hairs make me react."

"We could go outside," said Karen. She looked out the window. It was pouring rain. "We could take a walk or something," she said doubtfully.

"No, I'd better phone my mother to pick me

up," said Annette. "There are some pills at home that I can take so my eyes will stop tearing. I should have asked you about cats. You never mentioned them, and I didn't think of it."

Karen wondered when she would have had a chance to mention Peabody and Poughkeepsie. The subject wasn't something that came up in ordinary conversation. "Hello. I have two cats. Would you like to be my friend?" That Annette might have an allergic reaction to the cats had never occurred to her. She didn't know anyone else who had such an allergy.

During the ten minutes that the two girls were waiting for Annette's mother to pick her up, Karen stood about awkwardly. She didn't know if she should apologize or pretend that everything was normal. What was the etiquette for causing someone to have an allergic reaction? she wondered.

Though she had looked forward so eagerly to Annette's visit, she was very relieved when she was finally gone. Annette had not been in the Sossi house for even an hour, but Karen was exhausted from the tension. She sighed. Just my luck, she thought bitterly. Neither Sandy nor DeDe, the friends of Elaine and Aldo, was allergic to cats. But the friend that she brought home from school was.

She couldn't quite imagine that Roy Nevins would ever come visiting, but if he did, he would probably be allergic to cats too.

Sadly she went upstairs to her room. She would write a letter to one of her pen pals. At least she didn't have to worry about how they reacted in the presence of animals, she thought with a sigh.

She blinked away the tears that were in her eyes. No one has luck as bad as mine, she thought. The downstairs door slammed, and Aldo and Mrs. Sossi entered the house. Aldo ran up the stairs.

"Hey, where's your friend?" he asked. And then he noticed Karen's tears. "Are you crying?"

"No," sniffed Karen. "It's just an allergic reaction." She blew her nose.

"What are you allergic to?" asked Aldo, puzzled.

"Life," said Karen. "I've just discovered that I'm allergic to life."

8.

Karen Unpowders

Thanksgiving and report card time approached together. Elaine brought home a card filled with A's. Aldo had also done well. His report on Jeanne d'Arc had been one of the best in the class. Of the three Sossi children, only Karen had nothing to be thankful for when she saw her marks.

No matter what name she wrote on her test papers and homework papers, Carin or Karyn or Caren Sossi always had a failing grade. Each of her teachers had taken Karen aside and told her that she wasn't doing as well as she could be. They wanted to see her work harder and improve in the months ahead. But Karen was convinced that she would never do any better at all.

"Karen, this is the last evening I am going to let you baby-sit until your schoolwork improves," Mrs. Sossi reminded her as she left the house the Saturday following Thanksgiving.

The baby-sitting that Karen had dreamed about doing for months was now a constant source of contention at home. Her mother insisted that she was putting in too much time at other people's houses instead of sitting in her own and doing her homework. It was true that although she carried her school books with her, she never opened them when she was at the Collins' house. But she might not have spent that time doing schoolwork if she had been at home either. Having to do schoolwork at school was bad enough. At least, the home should be sacred, a place for enjoying oneself and not a place for suffering through English papers, math assignments, and science projects.

Karen put all thoughts of school out of her head as she entered the Collins' house. Taking care of Keith took all her energy. Even when he was asleep, she kept alert for any sound that he might make.

She liked baby-sitting even more than she had ever imagined. Of course, the best part was getting paid and seeing her savings grow. But she also liked being in charge. At home, her parents and Elaine were older and full of advice for her. Here she was the oldest and in command.

One other bonus she had received from baby-sitting was that she liked Keith. Once he got to know her, he was really very sweet. He had loads of energy, and he kept her busy, but she liked to listen to his baby speech. Each time she came, he knew new words. He had learned her name and liked to call her. "Karrrrren," he said.

"I've already tucked Keith into his crib," said Mrs. Collins, when Karen arrived. "He missed his nap today, and he seemed so tired that I decided not to have him stay up for you."

Karen was disappointed. She would have enjoyed playing with Keith for a while before his bedtime. However, sleep was important for a growing child. She would play with him next time—if her mother ever permitted her to have a next time.

Mr. and Mrs. Collins said good-bye to Karen and left. Karen had discovered that Mrs. Collins kept a whole shelf of cookbooks in the kitchen, and the last time she had been here, she had copied two new bread recipes from them. Karen began turning pages in one of the cookbooks. From upstairs, she could hear faint sounds coming from Keith's room. Sometimes when he was falling asleep, he would talk to himself. Karen listened to see if she could make out his words. He seemed to be making happy noises, laughing and babbling.

Karen turned another page and then another. Keith's laughter was getting louder. He sounded like Aldo when he was watching one of his favorite programs on TV. Karen wondered what could be so funny to a little child who was only two years old and who was lying in bed in the dark.

She tiptoed upstairs to peek into Keith's room. Maybe he had a toy in bed with him and it was amusing him. The hall light was on, and the door to Keith's room was open. Karen felt a tickle in her nose and tried to hold back a sneeze so she wouldn't distract him. She muffled the first sneeze, but she was overpowered by three more in quick succession. A sweet smell was making her sneeze and irritating her throat too. Through the doorway she could see Keith standing up in his bed. The room was full of white fumes. Karen started coughing. Could something be on fire? She rushed into

the room and turned on the overhead light.

Keith blinked his eyes as he adjusted to the brightness of the light. Karen's vision was obscured by the fumes in the air. The room wasn't hot. There didn't seem to be a fire. She noticed what looked like a white coating over everything in the room.

"Karrrrren," crowed Keith with delight. "Karrrr-ren." He held out a container that he was playing with.

Karen took it and sneezed as she came close to him. It was a talcum powder can. Mrs. Collins must have left it open on the chest near his bed. Keith had shaken the contents of the can into the air. His bed was covered with talcum powder and so was the floor. Karen rushed to open the window to air out the room and to make breathing easier.

"Oh, Keith, what have you done?" she asked in disbelief.

"Keif powder," he lisped, unable to pronounce his own name exactly. He stood looking very proud of his accomplishment.

Karen looked at him and the room and wondered if she should laugh or cry. Not only were the bed and the floor and every surface of the room covered with a coating of white powder, even

Keith's hair was full of powder. He looked like a little old white-haired man wearing diapers and a blanket sleeper.

"Keif powder," he said again.

"Karen unpowder," said Karen. She looked about and tried to decide where to begin. She couldn't believe that so much powder could have been in one little container.

"Where does your mother keep the vacuum cleaner?" she asked.

Keith smiled at her. Perhaps he understood her words, and perhaps he didn't. One never could be sure with a child his age. Karen left him in his crib, happily waving the empty talcum can, as she went out into the hallway and opened closets. At the bottom of the linen closet, she found the vacuum cleaner. As she began to clean the room, she felt a draft coming in from the window. She didn't want Keith to catch a cold, but she didn't think it was good for him to breathe in the talcum powder either. So she found his snowsuit in the closet and put it on him. Then she let him walk around as she shook out the sheet on his bed. Karen brushed the powder out of his hair as well as she could. He really needed a shampoo. She vacuumed off the chest, the shelves, and the floor.

"Keif powder," said Keith, yawning.

"Karen unpowder," said Karen, repeating her words. She found a washcloth in the linen closet and dampened it. She wiped around all the slats on Keith's bed.

"Keif powder," he said, rubbing his eyes.

Karen lifted him up and put him back into his crib.

"Karen unpowder," she said again. Noticing some powder that she had missed, she turned on the vacuum cleaner again and reached into the corner. The vacuum hose banged into the crib, and the bed shook slightly. She looked to see how Keith was reacting to all this activity. He was lying on his back with his thumb in his mouth and his eyes closed. "Don't fall asleep, Keith," she said. "I've got to take your snowsuit off."

Keith removed his thumb from his mouth and said softly, "Keif powder." Those were his last words of the evening. He was sound asleep. The vacuum cleaner was still on, and yet Keith was sleeping as soundly as if she were singing a lullaby.

Karen decided to leave his window half open and the snowsuit on him. She switched off the vacuum and looked over the room. A slightly sweet scent still hung in the air, but it was no longer overpowering enough to make her sneeze or choke.

By the time Karen had put the vacuum away and turned off the light in Keith's room, it was after nine thirty. She had spent well over an hour unpowdering Keith's room.

Exhausted, she sat down on the sofa, and the next thing she knew Mrs. Collins was standing over her. "Oh, I'm awfully sorry. I fell asleep," she apologized.

"That's all right. You must have been tired."

"I know, but I didn't mean to fall asleep. Not while I'm taking care of Keith."

"My husband and I fall asleep every night, even though we are taking care of Keith," said Mrs. Collins. "I'm sure you would have awakened had there been any emergency."

Karen nodded and took the money that Mrs. Collins handed her. "Oh, by the way," she said, as she walked to the door, "Keith is wearing his snowsuit."

"Snowsuit?" asked Mrs. Collins.

"Well, I thought it was a good idea since it got so drafty in his room."

"Drafty?"

"Yes, when I opened the window to clear the air."

"Air?" Mrs. Collins was puzzled.

"Yes," said Karen. "Keith powdered, and I un-powdered."

She saw Mrs. Collins' confused expression. "He took a can of talcum powder—" Karen began.

"Oh, no," said Mrs. Collins. "Not again. Did I leave the can of powder open and within his reach?"

Karen nodded her head.

"That's the second time. Oh, you poor thing. The room must be a mess."

"I vacuumed up most of it," said Karen.

"Karen, you're a jewel," said Mrs. Collins, hugging her.

Mr. Collins walked Karen back home. "Thanks for everything," he said. "Keith can be a handful. We really feel good when we know that you're taking care of him."

Karen remembered what her mother had said about baby-sitting earlier in the evening. She didn't want to tell Mr. Collins that she might not be permitted to sit again. So instead she said, "Thanks, Mr. Collins. I like Keith an awful lot too." She paused a moment. "Except, of course, when Keif powders."

Mr. Collins laughed. "Keith is really crazy about you," he said.

Just my luck, thought Karen, as she got ready for bed. A boy is finally crazy about me, and he is only two years old. But at that hour of the night, she was too tired to care.

9.

Homework Problems

On the first Monday in December, Karen got a zero in English because she didn't hand in an essay that was due. The teacher had said that they could write about anything they wanted, but there was nothing that Karen wanted to write about. She'd hoped that Mr. Dunn would forget to collect the papers and that she might have a brainstorm within the next twenty-four hours. How funny that she was able to think up a good idea to help Aldo, but when her own assignments were due, she had no ideas at all.

Mr. Dunn sent home a note asking Mrs. Sossi

to come to school and speak with him.

"I don't understand it," said her mother. "Why should you have trouble writing an essay for English? You like writing letters. An essay is just like a letter except that it is addressed to your teacher and not to a pen pal."

"No," said Karen. "Mr. Dunn is not my friend. I'm not writing a letter to him, and so I have nothing to say to him."

"Karen, it seems to me that there are two types of letter writers in the world. There are those who write 'Dear Friend, How are you? I am fine. Please write soon.' All you know from that kind of letter is that the writer is still alive. But you aren't like that at all. You are the second type, which is much rarer. I've seen letters that you've written to your pen pals. Some of them are like a story. If you can write that way when you don't have to write, then you should be able to write a page or two for your teacher."

Karen listened to her mother's lecture, but she didn't agree. Writing a paper for school and writing a letter were not the same. When she wrote on her fancy stationery, she felt good. Writing on the lined paper for school made her feel stiff and impersonal, just like the paper itself.

In the midst of their discussion of English papers, the phone rang. Mrs. Collins was calling to ask if Karen could baby-sit on Saturday evening. She couldn't have called at a worse time, Karen thought.

"I'm sorry, Mrs. Collins," her mother said on the telephone. "Karen won't be able to sit for the next few weeks. She has fallen behind in her schoolwork."

"You could have told her I was sick," shouted Karen, after Mrs. Sossi had hung up. "It's bad enough that you're so mean and aren't letting me baby-sit. Now she knows that I'm a dummy at school, too."

"Karen, you aren't a dummy," said Mrs. Sossi calmly. "But if you can't find time to get your work done for school, then you just don't have the time to spend at someone else's house. Schoolwork must come first."

"That's crazy," said Karen. "Schoolwork is to prepare me to get a job someday. And now I have a job and I'm making money, and you won't let me go to it. It isn't fair!" Tears of frustration were running down Karen's cheeks.

"You aren't going to be a baby-sitter all your life," said Mrs. Sossi. "When your schoolwork improves, then you can baby-sit and not a moment before."

"I hate school. I hate it, I hate it, and I hate you too," shouted Karen, running up the stairs to her bedroom and falling onto her bed. She wondered whom Mrs. Collins would call to take care of Keith instead of her. Soon he would forget who she was and cry if he saw her instead of shouting out "Karrrrren."

Karen lay on her bed weeping. Nobody was unluckier than she. It had taken her months to get a baby-sitting customer, and now she couldn't sit. She remembered Saturday evening when she had taken care of Keith. Even though the work had been hard, she had enjoyed herself.

Blowing her nose, she decided to write a letter to Keichi, her pen pal in Japan. She took out a piece of stationery and began writing. As she described her experience with Keith, she felt calmer and better than she had before. Letter writing always had that effect on her. Writing letters was like talking to a best friend, she thought, as she hunted through her desk for an airmail stamp to put on the envelope. She couldn't find one, so she couldn't mail the letter. She would have to go to the post office tomorrow.

The next afternoon Mrs. Sossi went to school to

116

meet with Mr. Dunn. Karen sat stiffly beside her mother as Mr. Dunn read out the list of dates when Karen had not handed in assignments. "I know some people find writing more difficult than others," he said, "but if she doesn't hand anything in to me, then she can't expect to pass."

"I don't understand it," said Mrs. Sossi. "Karen is a real writer. She writes letters all the time." She opened her pocketbook and handed a sheet of paper to Mr. Dunn. "Look at this," she said.

Karen looked at the paper with surprise. It was pink and had little animals walking along one edge. It was her stationery, and Mr. Dunn was reading the letter she had written yesterday to Keichi.

"That's my letter," Karen whispered to her mother, as Mr. Dunn began to read it. "It's private. You had no right to take it." Her face was flushed with anger and embarrassment. She didn't like the idea of both her mother and her teacher reading her private correspondence.

"Karen, this is very well written," said Mr. Dunn, looking up from the letter with amazement. "But your spelling is atrocious. Where does your pen pal live?"

"Japan," answered Karen in a whisper.

"Well, how do you expect the poor fellow to

understand you if you spell half of the words incorrectly? You really ought to look up words in the dictionary if you aren't certain of their spelling."

"Keichi makes mistakes in his letters to me all the time," said Karen, defending herself.

"Yes, but he is just learning English. You've been studying it since first grade. And if he is going to learn from your letters, you ought to teach him properly. It isn't as if you were studying Japanese. Then you would have an excuse for a mistake or two." Mr. Dunn smiled at Karen. "I would give this an A for content but only a B-minus for presentation. I'll tell you what," he said, opening his grade book. "We've just begun a new marking period. I'll put that A/B- down here as your first mark. So you are off to a wonderful start. Do you think you can keep it up? Just pretend that I am one of your pen pals."

"That's exactly what I told her," said Mrs. Sossi, nodding her head.

"I'll try," said Karen, which was not what she had said to her mother. Mr. Dunn seemed a whole lot nicer sitting in the English department office than he did in front of the class.

"Could I write on stationery instead of loose-leaf paper?"

"Would it make you feel better?" Mr. Dunn asked.

Karen nodded her head.

"Well, why not?" said Mr. Dunn. "I never get any pleasant mail these days anyhow. It will be a good change from all the bills." He smiled at Karen.

Karen and her mother got up to leave. Perhaps school wasn't so bad after all, Karen thought. They walked out into the hallway. School was over for the day, and the halls were empty. As they headed for the exit, Karen saw Ms. Drangle, her science teacher, coming toward them. She took a deep breath. She hoped her science teacher wasn't going to ask her mother to come in for a conference too.

But Ms. Drangle merely smiled and waved at Karen as they passed. "How's your science project coming?" she asked. Luckily, she didn't wait around for an answer.

"Science project? What science project?" asked Mrs. Sossi.

Karen shuddered. Surely no one had the luck that she did. It was all ups and downs.

"Tell me about this science project," said Mrs. Sossi, as they got into the car.

"Why do you have to bother me with that now?" asked Karen. "I just got an A in English, and you have to spoil it. Aren't you ever satisfied with me? I'm never going to be an all-A student like Elaine, so why don't you just leave me alone?"

"We both got that A in English," Mrs. Sossi reminded Karen. "You would never have gotten it if I hadn't showed your letter to Mr. Dunn."

"Well, even so, it was a lousy thing for you to do. You shouldn't touch my things," retorted Karen, remembering to be annoyed with her mother for the violation of her privacy.

"You're right," agreed her mother, "but in this case I think the end justified the means. It served its purpose. I won't do it again, and the next grade, whether it's in English or in science, is up to you. As for being an A student like Elaine, your father and I don't expect or want you to be like her. We like you for being Karen, and we like all the traits and characteristics that go with Karen. But you aren't being fair to yourself if you don't at least try to do as well as you can. Not everyone is an A student, but everyone can meet the assignments that they are given. And if you have been assigned to do a science project, then you had better start thinking about it right now."

Unfortunately, Mrs. Sossi was right. There was no getting around it. The deadline for the science project was approaching, and Karen had no idea what to do. Everyone in her family had suggestions.

Aldo said, "Why don't you study Peabody and Poughkeepsie? You could write about what cats eat, how much they sleep, and things like that."

121

"No," said Karen. "What could my class learn from that? Cats eat tuna fish and sleep a lot? Everyone already knows that."

"I got an A on my project last year," Elaine recalled. "I made charts of bacteria and showed the various types there are: bacilli, cocci, and spirilla. See? I still remember them."

"You sure used enough poster board," said Aldo. "I remember that."

"You're the poster board princess," said Karen. Elaine was always making huge poster board charts for her classes.

"Well, don't knock it. It works," said Elaine in a huff.

Karen's pleasure in her unexpected A in English quickly faded as she worried about a project for science. No one could be more miserable than she was, she decided. However, when she entered the house after school the following day, Aldo was crying. Even when he was a baby, Aldo hardly ever cried. She wondered what could be bothering him.

"What's up?" she asked her mother and Aldo, who were sitting together in the kitchen.

"Peabody is a murderer," wailed Aldo through his tears.

"What are you talking about?" asked Karen.

"He just walked into the house with a dead bird in his mouth," said Mrs. Sossi. "I managed to get it away from him."

"Are you crying for the bird?" asked Karen.

"I don't know," said Aldo softly. "I feel bad about the bird, but I feel bad about Peabody too. Why would he do a thing like that? He never killed a bird before."

"Well, he was an amateur up until now. Don't forget, we only moved here a few months ago, and he never had a shot at a bird until now," said Karen.

"It's part of nature," said Mrs. Sossi. "Cats always try to catch birds. Sometimes they succeed, and sometimes they don't. There isn't much that we can do about it."

"But it's all my fault," said Aldo.

"How could it be your fault?" asked Mrs. Sossi.

"I forgot to feed Peabody and Poughkeepsie before I went to school this morning. I was late, and I rushed out of the house, and I didn't even think of them until the middle of the morning when I was going to Phys. Ed."

"Where's the bird now?" asked Karen, curious about the victim.

"I put it outside in the garbage can," said Mrs. Sossi.

"She wouldn't even let me have a funeral and bury it," said Aldo, wiping his eyes.

"Better not to," said his mother. "I don't want the cats to dig it up. This way the matter is over and forgotten."

"Not forgotten," said Aldo, blowing his nose.

"Well, perhaps it won't happen again," Mrs. Sossi said.

She was wrong. That very evening, when Elaine was getting ready for bed, she let out a scream. Everyone came running into her room. "What's the matter?" asked her father anxiously.

"Look!" Elaine shouted, pointing to the floor of her closet.

Everyone crowded to look inside. There was a dead bird on the floor.

"What are you shouting for?" asked Mr. Sossi, picking up the cause of the excitement in a couple of tissues. "Don't tell me you are afraid of this."

"I'm not afraid," said Elaine, laughing. "It just surprised me. How would you like to find a corpse in your closet when you are getting undressed?"

Everyone laughed except Aldo.

Two days later there was a third bird. This one was brought into the house by Poughkeepsie and was still alive. Mrs. Sossi let out a shriek of surprise, and Poughkeepsie dropped his prey. The bird fluttered from the kitchen to the living room, leaving a trail of small feathers behind it.

Mrs. Sossi managed to rescue the bird before either of the cats were able to catch it again. That evening the family had a discussion on the subject as they were eating supper.

"I know I fed them enough," said Aldo. "I've been very careful and even have given them extra so they wouldn't go after the birds."

"Perhaps we shouldn't let them outside anymore," said Mrs. Sossi. "Soon there won't be any birds left in all of New Jersey with these two gangsters of ours on the loose."

"Don't be silly," said Mr. Sossi. "There are thousands of birds flying about, and if these birds were caught, they were probably sick or weak or something That's what is known as survival of the fittest."

Mrs. Sossi changed the subject. "Karen, have you found a topic for your science project yet?" she asked.

Karen shook her head.

"I hope you're thinking about it," she said warningly.

"That's all I think about," Karen complained. "Soon I'll be having nightmares about it."

Early Friday morning, when everyone was rushing about getting ready for school, Peabody brought another bird into the house. Aldo took the death of each small bird very hard. He acted as if he had known the bird personally and as if he had been betrayed by the cats. How could these creatures that he had known and loved all his life have suddenly turned into murderers?

Karen watched as Aldo gingerly picked up the corpse of the dead bird and put it into the garbage. Suddenly she had an idea. Maybe she could write about cats and birds for science. She could keep track of the number of birds that the cats had caught and study the birds and make graphs and charts about her findings.

"Do you think the cold weather has something to do with this business of the birds?" she asked Aldo. "Perhaps it brings out the killer instinct in the cats, or it makes the birds more sluggish?"

"Peabody and Poughkeepsie haven't got killer instincts," said Aldo, defending the cats. "They don't eat the birds. They just catch them and play

with them. But they are too rough, and they acci-
dentally kill them."

Karen wasn't so sure about that, but she didn't
want to upset Aldo by telling him so.

"Perhaps we should keep the cats inside," said
Mrs. Sossi, repeating her suggestion of the evening
before.

"Oh, no," Karen protested. "I want them to go
outside. I want to see how many birds they kill.
What they do would make a good science project."

"That's a terrible project," said Aldo.

"Well, maybe the cats won't kill anything anymore," said Karen. "But I want to keep score of the
birds in the area and the number of cats. And
besides you were the one who suggested that I
write about Peabody and Poughkeepsie in the first
place."

"That's not what I meant," said Aldo. "What
you want to do is disgusting," he said, and he
banged his fist on the table for emphasis. In doing
so, he knocked over his glass of milk. He had made
his point and soaked half the mats on the table as
well.

"Well, it's disgusting to have to do a science
project," said Karen, gathering her books together
to go off to school.

"If you do that for your project, I won't ever speak to you again," threatened Aldo.

Elaine started to laugh. "This must be the only family in the world that needs a United Nations mediator to keep peace on the subject of science projects."

"I'd be just as glad not to do any science project at all," said Karen.

"Just a minute," said Mrs. Sossi, wiping up the spilled milk. "Maybe Karen can find a solution to the problem of cats that kill birds and use it for her science project."

"I don't want her writing about Peabody and Poughkeepsie killing birds," said Aldo.

"I don't have to use their names," said Karen.

"The names have been changed to protect the innocent," said Elaine. Then she added, "Some families have black sheep. We have black cats. Or you could say we have a skeleton in our closet—a bird skeleton, that is."

"Stop joking about this," said Aldo. He was close to tears. "I know Peabody and Poughkeepsie can't help themselves. It's part of their nature to kill birds, but I don't think we should write about it and talk about it with others. We should keep it private."

"OK, OK," said Karen, looking at the clock. She was afraid she would miss the bus to school in addition to all her other troubles. "I don't care. I won't do it. Just find me another science project."

She ran out the door.

Mrs. Sossi ran after her to give her the lunch bag that she had left on the kitchen table. At least it hadn't gotten soaked in the spilled milk.

10.

Searching for a Science Project

Christmas was coming. Aldo went about the house interviewing all the family. "What do you want me to get you for Christmas?" he asked everyone.

Elaine wanted a leather shoulder bag that she had seen in a shop window in town. She didn't think that Aldo would be able to buy it for her, but she told him about it just the same so that he could pass the word on to their parents. Little brothers had their uses. She even gave her old bag to Karen and put a shabby older one back into use. It was frayed and sorry looking and would surely convince

131

her mother to buy her a new one.

Karen was pleased with her new acquisition, but she was not taking much pleasure in thinking about the approaching holiday. In the first place, she had been forbidden to do any cooking until she had completed a science project.

"No cooking!" she had screamed. "I wanted to make fruitcakes for Christmas gifts."

"No cakes, no bread, no experimenting in the kitchen until you get an experiment for school first," said Mrs. Sossi firmly.

"It's not fair! You eat all of whatever I make. You all like everything. So why shouldn't I bake or cook just because I haven't done my project?"

"Your mind should be on one thing and one thing only," said Mrs. Sossi.

So when Aldo asked Karen what she wanted for Christmas, she said, "I want a science project." Then she sighed. "But it will be too late." Her project was due on the Friday before school broke for the ten-day vacation.

"What sorts of things are the others in your class doing?" Mr. Sossi asked Karen one night at supper, when the subject of the elusive science project came up again.

"No one knows. Everyone is keeping their project a big secret so that no one will copy," Karen complained.

"I remember how it was," said Elaine. "I don't think even the CIA could have penetrated the secrecy of the science projects last year." She laughed.

"What's the CIA?" asked Aldo.

"Central Intelligence Agency," Elaine answered. "It's a fancy name for spies."

"Maybe if you wore a disguise you could find out," said Aldo. "You could make yourself look as if you were in a different grade or something."

"You all think this is a joke," complained Karen. "The science grade depends on this project." She didn't say so, but she was more upset about the continued loss of her baby-sitting jobs and the kitchen's being off limits than she was about her science project.

"Poughkeepsie brought another dead bird into the house," Mrs. Sossi informed her husband. Aldo no longer burst into tears at the sight of the dead birds, but he still felt bad about them.

"You know," said Elaine, "I think I read somewhere that when a pet brings a dead animal into the house, he's bringing a gift to his owner. So really Poughkeepsie and Peabody probably think they are bringing us Christmas presents every time they bring one of those birds inside."

"The best present would be no more presents," said Aldo.

Mr. Sossi changed the subject to raking the leaves. "Whose turn is it to bag them?" he asked. Elaine, Karen, and Aldo had been taking turns. Since this was their first autumn in the suburbs, the job of raking the falling leaves had been fun at first. Now that they had each done it for a while, however, they had had enough.

"It's endless," Elaine complained. "Even as I'm raking, more leaves are falling."

"Why don't you write about why the leaves fall off the trees every year?" Mrs. Sossi suggested, turning to Karen. No matter what they were talking about, the subject always seemed to return to the science project.

Mrs. Collins phoned to ask if Karen would be permitted to sit during the vacation. Karen looked expectantly at her parents.

"If you haven't handed in a science project, you are going to have to spend the entire vacation working on one," her mother warned. "Schoolwork comes first!"

So, even though Christmas was approaching,

Karen was feeling miserable. One evening she was looking through the books she had borrowed from the public library: *Science for Young Scientists*, *Make a Laboratory out of Your Bathroom* and *Science under Your Feet*.

Mrs. Sossi sat down next to Karen and looked through the books with her. "Couldn't you do this?" She was pointing to an experiment.

Karen read the description of it. The experiment involved litmus paper and weather reporting. "Too late," said Karen. "You need three or four weeks for this project." Karen sighed. "That's what I like about cooking," she said. "You make something, and an hour or so later you eat it. Not this business of working for three weeks to get results."

"Don't ever take up knitting or needlepoint," said Mrs. Sossi. "It took me three months to make you that Irish-style sweater." Mrs. Sossi thought a moment. Then she added, "Some foods take a long time to prepare. Cheese and wine need time to age. Why don't you do a report on something like that?"

"I'd love to bring a bottle of wine to my class and get everyone a little drunk," Karen said, giggling. But she vetoed her mother's suggestion. She did not want to do a report on cheese or wine.

"Well, you're not getting anything done by moping about and just turning pages in these books," said Mrs. Sossi. "Why don't you bake some fresh bread for us?"

"Do you really mean it?" Karen asked in amazement. It was more than two weeks since the kitchen had been declared off limits except for eating and dish washing.

The thought of being in the kitchen and quietly kneading some bread dough filled Karen with pleasure. She always felt a sense of peace and well-being when she cooked, but especially when she made bread. All her senses enjoyed the activity: touch when she kneaded the dough, smell as it baked, sight when she looked at the finished product, hearing when her family praised her work, and, of course, taste when she took the first bite of the bread. No wonder bread is considered the staff of life, Karen thought, as she began measuring the ingredients. It satisfies all of one's senses!

Aldo came into the kitchen as Karen was kneading the dough. "It really is like magic how that glop turns into bread," he said, as he watched her. "It looks as though it should taste awful."

Karen laughed and kept on kneading.

Elaine walked into the kitchen. "Oh, great!" she

exclaimed. "You may not be such a good student at school, but I bet if you ran the school cafeteria, nobody would have any complaints."

While the dough was rising, Karen returned to her homework. She felt so relaxed that she didn't even mind doing her math problems. Ever since the Halloween party, she had become fond of Mrs. Nesbitt, and even if she got the problems wrong, she didn't want to disappoint her by not doing the assigned work.

Karen thought about the bread. What had Aldo said? Making bread is like magic. That was what Ms. Drangle had said about science. "Science is the answer to everything that we can't understand —all the things that seem like magic—such as why a bird can fly or a baby is born or a television set shows pictures or a calculator does math problems."

"I've got it! I've got it!" Karen screamed.

"Oh, no!" Aldo came running. "Not another bird," he cried out.

"Where is it?" called Mr. Sossi, jumping up from his chair in front of the television.

"Here, I'll take it," Mrs. Sossi offered, coming with some paper towels in her hand.

"Boy, you make more noise than me, and yet

you complained when I found that bird in my closet and screamed!" shouted Elaine, coming from her room.

They all stood in Karen's room looking about.

"Well, where is it?" asked Mr. Sossi, eager to return to his program.

"Where is what?" asked Karen, surprised to see her room full of her family.

"The bird!" said Aldo, Elaine, and Mr. and Mrs. Sossi in unison.

"What bird?" asked Karen.

"The one you're shouting about."

Karen looked confused. "I'm not shouting. There's no bird," she said.

"You said you've got it. We all heard you," said Mrs. Sossi.

"I've got something better than a bird." Karen laughed. "I just got an idea for a science project!"

"You're not going to report on Peabody and Poughkeepsie, are you?" asked Aldo. His mind was still on the bird that he had thought was in Karen's room.

"Nope!" Karen said, grinning.

"What is it then?" asked Aldo doubtfully.

Karen looked at her family. They were all waiting to hear her idea. Suddenly she looked at the clock. "Come on. I'll show you," she said.

She ran down the stairs with everyone following her. Even Peabody and Poughkeepsie had emerged from hidden nooks to join them.

Karen opened the oven door and showed them the bowl of dough rising inside. "This is going to be my science project," she said.

"Bread?" asked Aldo. "How can that be your project?"

"Silly," said Karen. "You're the one who gave me the idea. Well, actually, it was you and Mom both. You said bread was like magic, and Mom said that I should do a project on a food that needs time like wine or cheese. Anyhow, bread is like magic. And I'm going to explain how the magic works."

"That's a wonderful idea," said Mrs. Sossi. "You could even give everyone a taste of the finished loaf."

"You could do it the way Julia Child does on TV and bring all the ingredients and show how each step is done," added Mr. Sossi.

Then everyone had suggestions. Elaine found a piece of poster board in her closet and offered it to Karen. "You could list the ingredients on this and draw pictures of each process," she said.

"You'll have to explain about yeast and how it

functions to make the bread rise," said Mrs. Sossi. Once again the old set of the encyclopedia was going to come in handy.

"This will be as good as John Dark," said Aldo. "I'm sure glad that you're not writing about Peabody and Poughkeepsie!"

11.

Ms. Drangle Jangles

Karen spent the next afternoon working on her chart and gathering together all the ingredients that she would need to take to school. After supper, she didn't even ask to watch television. She just kept on working. Her only interruption was a telephone call from Mrs. Collins, who wanted her to baby-sit on New Year's Eve. "I know it's a special holiday, so I'm willing to pay two dollars an hour," said Mrs. Collins.

"I don't know if I can," said Karen, thinking of her mother's ban on baby-sitting.

"Please, Karen. I'll pay you three dollars an hour!"

Karen couldn't believe her ears. She rushed to plead with her mother.

"Since your science project will be done, I don't have any objections," said Mrs. Sossi. "But you'll have to be sure to keep up-to-date with all of your work in the future," she warned, as Karen rushed back to the telephone.

Some days life could be wonderful, Karen thought.

Ms. Drangle had had her students draw lots way back in October. In this way, they had each been given a date to report on their science project to the class. Now that Karen had a project, the Friday before vacation seemed to her the perfect date.

On Friday morning, Karen set her alarm clock for five thirty. She got up and dressed quietly. The sky outside her window looked like midnight. Thank goodness, tomorrow I can sleep as late as I want, she thought, as she put on her clothes in the chilly bedroom.

She tiptoed down to the kitchen so as not to wake any of the rest of her family. As she set out the ingredients for school, she almost tripped.

Looking down, she saw that both Peabody and Poughkeepsie were underfoot. Despite the small bell that each of them wore on his collar, she had not heard them. "You're so quiet, I didn't know you were here," she complained aloud to the two cats. "Is that how you sneak up on those poor defenseless birds?"

She mixed the yeast with warm water and let it dissolve. She measured out the flour, butter, and milk that she would need for her bread. Karen's plan was to take a bowl of bread dough into the class and show them what it looked like at that stage. "The glop stage," Aldo called it. She would be just like Julia Child showing each of the steps. Of course, the exposure to the cold air would prevent the dough from rising properly, but Karen wanted to show her class the texture of the dough at first. And then she would explain the scientific reasons that the dough increased in size and why the yeast worked the way it did. "You're going to do a snow job on your teacher," Elaine had said. "Just because you're a good cook, your teacher will think you are a good science student too."

The rest of the family began to waken. Karen listened to the morning sounds as she kneaded her dough. From the bathroom, she could hear her father's electric shaver. The radio was on in Elaine's room. "They're predicting snow," she shouted to the rest of the family.

Mrs. Sossi came down to the kitchen and put on a pot of coffee. "I'll drive you to school this morning," she offered to Karen. "I don't think you'll ever make it on the bus with all your paraphernalia."

"What's paraphernalia?" asked Aldo. "Is it a kind of bread, like pumpernickle?"

"It's all that stuff," said Mrs. Sossi, pointing to the two loaves neatly wrapped in aluminum foil, the large bowl of dough, and the other ingredients that Karen was also planning to take to school.

"Oh, great," said Karen. "In that case, I'm going to take a jar of jam too."

"Why jam?" asked Mrs. Sossi.

"Since the bread is rescuing her from a jam, she is bringing jam with the bread," quipped Mr. Sossi, entering the kitchen.

Everyone laughed. The solution of Karen's science crisis was a relief felt not only by Karen but by the entire family.

Luckily for Karen, she had science first period. Most days this schedule wasn't any reason for rejoicing at all. But today she was eager to give her

146

report and have it done. The rest of the day would be a snap.

One other classmate was giving his report this morning too. Karen was scheduled after Peter London, who told how astronauts could hear each other in space. He explained how sound could travel in gases, liquids, and solids. "Sound travels at a speed of about 330 meters per second in air at zero degrees Celsius. That's equivalent to 750 miles per hour," Peter explained. "And the colder it is, the slower sound travels," he added.

Karen sat only half listening. She was beginning to feel nervous. She didn't like to get up in front of the class. She fidgeted in her seat and looked at Ms. Drangle. Whenever her science teacher moved, she made a jingling sound today. She was wearing a necklace that seemed to be made out of coins, which hit against one another as she walked about the classroom.

"Sound travels through water four times faster than through air," Peter said. Karen tried to imagine Ms. Drangle wearing her necklace and a bathing suit and swimming underwater. For miles and miles other swimmers would hear the jingling, jangling of the coins.

Karen's mind drifted farther and farther away

from the science classroom. She wasn't sure if the purpose of these projects was for the students to learn from one another or if it was for them to organize their thinking or what. She knew she had picked up only a few facts during the course of the past few weeks while her classmates had been reporting. Mostly her notebook was full of doodles that had nothing to do with science. She wondered if she would learn even one useful fact before the reporting was over.

Peter finished up his report. For the past few minutes, he had been hitting glasses of water with a spoon and getting sounds. The purpose of that, thought Karen to herself, is to learn how to get attention in a restaurant.

"All right, Peter, that was very interesting," said Ms. Drangle. She made some notes in her black grade book. Everyone waited. They knew that those notes were the basis of the half-term grade.

Peter sighed with relief. He was finished. Now Karen's turn had come.

Karen stood up and cleared her throat. She had been practicing an opening sentence, since the beginning was always the hardest. "I have something in a little envelope for you to see," she said. Whereupon, she opened an envelope and poured the contents into a saucer. Then she began to walk slowly around the classroom so that everyone would have a chance to investigate the tan grains on the dish.

"Is it animal, vegetable, or mineral?" asked Roy Nevins.

"What do you think it is?" asked Karen. Of course, she knew the answer because she had read all about yeast in the encyclopedia.

Annette Rubin raised her hand. "It must be metal because it looks like filings," she suggested.

Karen grinned and shook her head. "Nope," she said.

"No fair," said Peter. "You should tell us what we're looking at."

Karen turned to look at Ms. Drangle.

"Tell them what it is," she said. "They probably have never seen that substance before."

"It's yeast," said Karen.

"Yeast is alive," said Peter knowingly. "So it must be animal."

"Nope," said Karen. "It's vegetable."

"Vegetable!" said Annette, looking again at the grains on the plate. "Give me green peas any day."

"This yeast that I bought at the supermarket contains a mass of tiny, one-celled plants. They are the simplest kind of plants and belong to a group known as fungi," Karen explained.

"Mushrooms are fungi," called out Peter.

"That's right," said Karen. "But we don't put mushrooms in bread. Instead, we use these little grains of yeast, which are actually made by mixing yeast cells and cornmeal."

"But how does it turn into bread?" someone called out.

Karen opened a bag of flour and began pouring some into a bowl. "Three cups of this fine white powder, mixed with just a couple of spoons of this lumpier tan powder, which is the yeast, are the two main ingredients of bread," she explained. "Warm liquid starts the yeast growing. Yeast cells give off chemicals called 'enzymes' when they are growing, and these enzymes attack the starch in the flour and change it to sugar. The sugar is then changed to alcohol and carbon dioxide gas. You know how sometimes bread has air holes in it? They are caused by the bubbling of the gas, which makes the bread rise."

"Carbon dioxide is poison," said Annette.

"I thought kids our age couldn't have alcohol," said Roy. "You mean to say that there is alcohol in bread?"

"No," said Karen. "When the bread is baked in the oven, the alcohol is evaporated and the yeast plants are destroyed by the heat."

Then Karen lifted the cloth that had been covering the bowl of completed dough. "This is what dough looks like," she said, walking about the room once again to let everyone have a good look.

"It sure doesn't look or smell like bread," called out Roy.

"My brother says it's glop," said Karen, and everyone laughed. "But after it has finished rising and I put it into the oven and let it bake, it becomes bread. Yesterday I put two pans of the glop into the oven, and this is what happened." As she spoke, Karen removed the two loaves of bread that she had kept hidden in a shopping bag. She began unwrapping one of the loaves, and everyone gasped.

"It looks like real bread," said one of the boys.

"It tastes like real bread too," said Karen proudly. She was enjoying herself very much. She turned to Ms. Drangle. "Would it be all right if I gave everyone a slice of bread?" she asked.

Ms. Drangle nodded her head and came toward the front of the room, jingling and jangling as she walked. Karen had a knife in her paraphernalia, and now she began slicing the bread. "It's even better with jam," she said, pointing to the jar of jam that she had with her.

"Why not?" said Ms. Drangle. "This is like a

real holiday party we're having." She smiled at Karen.

Soon everyone was chewing on a slice of home-made bread. There were lots of questions. "Why is some bread called whole wheat and some white? Isn't all bread made of wheat?"

Karen was able to answer all the questions, especially the ones that weren't very scientific. Many of the students wanted to know if bread was hard to make, and if it cost a lot of money, and if it took a lot of time.

Usually Karen was silent in class. She had probably spoken no more than a dozen words since the first day of school and those only when she had been called upon by Ms. Drangle, despite her not having raised her hand. This morning she felt strange to be up in front and leading the discussion, but she was having fun too.

Ms. Drangle helped distribute seconds to everyone. There was nothing left but a few crumbs. Her jingling added to the happy mood in the room. They really felt as though they were having a party.

Suddenly as she listened to Ms. Drangle's necklace, Karen thought of something. She stared hard at her teacher and wondered why such a simple idea hadn't occurred to her earlier.

"Does it?" Lisa asked.

"Does it what?" asked Karen. She hadn't heard the question. She had been too busy listening to Ms. Drangle's necklace and realizing that if cats had *several* bells attached to their collars they probably wouldn't catch any more birds. Peter had said that the colder it is, the slower sound travels. No wonder Peabody and Poughkeepsie had suddenly succeeded in becoming murderers when the weather turned cold. She would buy them new collars for Christmas, she thought.

"Does all bread have yeast in it?" Lisa asked.

Karen knew the answer to that question. She explained to the class about baking soda and baking powder and how they worked.

The bell rang. The science period was over, and the time had come to leave. Karen gathered her bowls and ingredients together. "That was an excellent report," said Ms. Drangle. "The idea was very creative. I didn't know that you were so interested in cooking," she said, smiling at her student.

"Oh, I love cooking," said Karen. "I want to become a chef when I grow up."

"I think you're a chef already if you can make such good bread," said Ms. Drangle. "My cousin studied at the CIA for a while. She is interested in cooking too."

"The CIA? Those are spies. Does she spy on

other cooks for their recipes?" Karen asked in amazement.

Ms. Drangle laughed. "This is a different CIA," she explained. "Culinary Institute of America. It's a wonderful cooking school. Perhaps you can go there after you finish high school."

Karen beamed. She would love to study at the CIA.

The rest of the day should have dragged as it usually did before a vacation. But Karen found herself the center of attention all day long. Her bread-making ability had given her a new status among her classmates.

Annette Rubin passed Karen a note in math class asking if Karen would come to *her* house and give her a cooking lesson during the vacation. Karen looked over to Annette and nodded her head in acceptance. Teaching Annette would be a lot of fun.

Annette passed her a second note. "Please give me your phone number," it said. Karen wrote the number down on the paper. Then she wrote her name next to it in big letters. "K-A-R-E-N." She didn't even think of the alternate spellings. Today being just plain old Karen felt very good.

At lunchtime, Roy and Peter came over to the

table where Karen was eating to report that her bread was much better than the bread in their sandwiches. Karen blushed. She had heard that the way to a man's heart was through his stomach. Perhaps that applied to eighth-grade boys as well.

Finally dismissal time came. All the students ran to their buses, eager for the holidays to begin. None of the teachers had assigned homework. Karen had difficulty managing all her packages. Although she no longer had the two loaves of bread or the dough, which she had disposed of because it was ruined from exposure to the morning air, she still had the bowl, the bag of flour, and all the other things that she had taken out of her locker. All lockers always had to be completely emptied before school vacations. With her arms full, she awkwardly squeezed into a seat next to another girl.

Only after a couple of minutes had passed and the bus was moving along did Karen realize that she was sitting on the pocketbook that Elaine had given her. She took it out from under her and opened the bag to check on the contents.

"Oh, look," she said, as she showed her seatmate. "I sat on my pocketbook, and I broke the little mirror inside."

"Are you superstitious?" asked the girl. "They say it can bring you seven years of bad luck."

"With my luck, it will be fourteen," said Karen. But as she sat in her seat gathering the little shards of the mirror together, she realized that what she'd said wasn't true at all.

Her bad luck this fall she had brought on herself. The broken chain letters had seemed a good reason for her misfortunes, but she knew now that she could only blame herself. She had been lazy and careless. How could she expect to pass in school if she didn't even try to hand in her assignments on time? Good luck was like making bread. It took time and effort.

"No, I take that back," said Karen to her seatmate. "I'm not superstitious at all. In fact, even though the mirror is broken, I think I'm going to be having some good luck now." She smiled to herself. She was sure of it.

About the Author

Johanna Hurwitz did not write *Tough-Luck Karen* as an autobiography. However, she admits that like Karen she 1) was a poor science student, 2) likes to bake bread, 3) has two cats. Born and educated in New York, Johanna Hurwitz lives on Long Island, New York with her husband Uri, and their teenage children, Nomi and Beni. Other titles by Johanna Hurwitz available from Scholastic in Apple® Paperback editions are *Aldo Applesauce*, and *What Goes Up Must Come Down* (hardcover title: *The Law of Gravity*), and in a Scholastic paperback edition, *All About Aldo* (hardcover title: *Much Ado About Aldo*).

About the Illustrator

Diane de Groat was born in New Jersey and received a Bachelor of Fine Arts degree from Pratt Institute. Since 1971 she has worked as a free-lance designer and illustrator. Her work has been exhibited at the Society of Illustrators' Gallery and the Art Directors' Club. She lives with her husband and daughter in Yonkers, New York.